"A swashbuckling adventure story seen through a mid-century cinematic lens. These terse, pulpy pages transport you from the seedy shipyards of Houston, Texas to the teeming jungles of Costa Rica. Along the journey I fell in love with with the heroes, was riveted by the plot's prison breaks and puma strikes, and was delighted by the tale's unlikely and wholly-satisfying conclusion. As captivating as fireworks."
~ Nikhil Melnechuk, Executive Director, Bowery Poetry

"Buckle up, the Bridge To Alta Vista is a perilous, wild epic odyssey that takes place in the 1960's into the the 1970's from Houston, Texas to the Costa Rica jungles. It will entrance your mind with love and fate, yet you'll feel the danger and loss. The chance encounters with the authorities, Boruca Indians, boa constrictors, crocodiles and criminals leave you wanting more, page after page!"
~ Melissa Jackson, Winding Roads Productions

"With the Bridge To Alta Vista, Gerald Thompson has given us an adventure packed with so many fun twists and turns and unexpected treats, Tom Sawyer himself might be envious of what Thompson has pulled off with his first novel. Thompson's intrinsic sense of storytelling and the world he has created is a verifiable delight to get lost in."
~ John Buffalo Mailer

BRIDGE TO

ALTA

VISTA

Gerald Thompson

CKBooks

For inquiries about Gerald Thompson's works, email him at: jerrythomp@gmail.com · Website: geraldthompsonauthor.com

Names: Thompson, Gerald, 1957-
Title: Bridge to Alta Vista / Gerald Thompson.
Description: New Glarus, WI : CKBooks, [2017]
Identifiers: ISBN 9780988199354 (softcover) | ISBN 9780988199361 (ebook)
Subjects: LCSH: Ex-convicts–Fiction. | Man-woman relationships–Fiction. | Drug dealers–Costa Rica–Fiction. | Escapes–Costa Rica–Fiction. | LCGFT: Thrillers (Fiction)
Classification: LCC PS3620.H6644 B75 2017 (print) | LCC PS3620. H6644 (ebook) | DDC 813/.6–dc23

Published, designed and edited by
CKBooks Publishing
P.O. Box 214, New Glarus, WI 53574
ckbookspublishing.com

This book is dedicated to my mother,
Barbara McCabe Thompson.
As I was growing up when I told her I had
nothing to do, she always said,
"Go outside and play."

෨

In memory of my father,
Raymond Brown Thompson

Costa Rica

*Home to the Wanted
and the Unwanted*

CHAPTER ONE

BANG, BANG YOU'RE DEAD

Houston, Texas, 1966

The sun was about to set, casting the darkest of shadows around the four posts of Billie's bed. The sound of footsteps approaching the bedroom keyed Billie into making final mental preparations. He held his breath as the latch clicked and the door to his room opened. Billie was ready. Enough was enough. Billie made the decision to face his fears, fight the monster, kill or be killed. He had what he needed to defend himself, at the very least, or to go on the offensive to finish the bastard off. He was prepared to do whatever it would take.

"Take your pants down and bend over," Jake demanded with a smirk as he walked over and clicked on the nightstand lamp so he could see clearly.

Billie hesitated but complied as he always had. In the past, he would not say a word, in fear of his life, but tonight he would endure the pain and humility for the last time. This would be it. Billie was bound and determined to end his living nightmare right here, right now.

Jake pulled down his shorts and walked over to Billie, readying to enter him forcefully.

Billie tried to stand. "Stop it! Right now, stop it!" Billie yelled out as loud as he could.

Jake didn't listen; he continued his advance on Billie, the demons in his sick, twisted mind encouraging him.

"Shut the fuck up before the damn neighbors hear you squealing like a pussy," Jake said, pushing him back down. "Keep your mouth shut or I will whip you with the belt real good. You're getting too old for me, my Billie boy. You're not my sweet sugar baby anymore. This will be the last time with you anyway. You might as well enjoy it," Jake said confidently.

"I've had enough of this you sick fucker. Get the hell off of me NOW, old man," Billie said in a stronger, more threatening voice.

Billie rose up off his knees, twisting to turn around to confront the evil bastard face to face.

"Shut the hell up, Billie, stay still. I am almost there," Jake commanded pushing Billie's head down.

With unwavering determination Billie's fury rose to

full strength, instantly shedding his boyhood and taking on the confidence of a man.

"Did you hear me? I am telling you for the last time, get off me right now, you asshole," Billie screamed out as he stood tall, pushing Jake back. "Enough is enough, you shit-head."

"What the fuck are you talking about? Turn around and get back on your knees," Jake howled. He grabbed Billie's shoulder, forcing him to turn around and face forward.

Swinging his right arm around in a full circle, Billie was able to knock Jake onto the bed. While Jake rolled off the bed, crawled up on his knees, and stood up, Billie reached between the mattresses for the semi-automatic Glock he had stolen from Jake's bedroom a week earlier. He stood to face his prick of a father, pulled the slide back to engage a bullet into the chamber, and pointed the barrel directly at the monster's forehead. Jake looked at Billie in total bewilderment, shock, and disbelief.

"Give me my goddamn gun, Billie or I will shove it up your ass." He held out an open palm. "How in the hell did you get your filthy, thieving hands on that, anyway?" Jake demanded.

The look in his stepfather's eyes chilled the air in the room. The pistol in Billie's hand started to shake. Billie was on the verge of losing control. The revolver almost fell from his hand as the trembling increased uncontrollably. Billie put both hands on the butt of the gun and squeezed as hard as he could. Then he leaned down and wiped the cold sweat from his forehead on the sleeve of his shirt. Regaining control, he mustered enough internal strength to stand tall and do what had to be done or lose his life in the process.

"You are a bastard, Jake, a real son of a bitch. I am going to send you off to hell where you all belong." Billie's voice was shrill but in control.

"Give it to me now, little man. Give me the goddamn gun this instant. I am your father, so that makes you my little bitch," Jake blurted out.

"I am not your bitch anymore, and you are not a father," Billie shouted back.

Jake lunged for the Glock, grabbing Billie's wrist as they hit the ground and rolled on the hardwood floor. Jake was powerful and Billie could feel his grip on the gun slipping. Hope of escaping the sick life he knew was about to drift away. Billie briefly saw an image of his mother flash through his mind. She was weeping and reaching out to him. Her voice a distant sound. "Billie, Billie, my sweet little Billie." The vision disappeared, her voice gone as quickly as it came.

"Give me strength, mother," Billie whispered.

Quickly and decisively Billie rolled over, unpinning himself from Jake's weight. Then he tightened his grip on the gun. Firmly and without reservation, he pulled the trigger twice, each shot piercing Jake's forehead just above the eye sockets. In that one surreal, lonely blink in time, the only thing Billie remembered following that night of horror were the two loud bangs, sweet music to his ears.

Bang…bang…you're dead. Bang…bang…you're dead. A simple, hideous nursery rhyme repeating itself over and over in Billie's head.

"The monster's dead. The monster's dead. Yeah, yeah, the monster's dead."

⁜

Having killed his stepfather at age fourteen, Billie was tried as a child in the Texas court. Billie was sentenced to seven years at The Youth Village: a maximum security, juvenile detention mental health facility where he would stay until he turned twenty-one. He would get out on his twenty-first birthday as long as he behaved properly and wasn't considered a threat. Soon after Billie was sentenced and incarcerated as a juvenile offender, he was assigned a therapist, Doctor Jean Scott. She spent most of her time working with Billie on his anger issues. They talked, they shared emotions, they slowly connected. Over time, every sick detail of his ordeal was exposed. Billie told her everything, including the nightmare, his sick repeating dream of the night he killed his father. He told her how many times he felt like he wanted to die. How he wanted to kill himself.

Doctor Scott knew exactly what he was feeling. She had experienced those same blameful thoughts when she was a young girl. She had grown up with an abusive father too. She was proud that Billie had the courage to stand up to his father, to face the monster and even kill him, though she would never tell him that. She never could do it to her old man, even though she thought about it every single day.

Doctor Scott had a special place in her heart for Billie; she knew what demons he was facing and would continue to face for the rest of his life. His personality was shaped by hatred and anger for what his stepfather had done to him.

Billie made progress some days, taking one step forward and regressed on others, taking two steps backwards. He was making inroads, climbing out from his hellhole slowly but steadily. Billie had a good soul, she could tell. Doctor Scott thought Billie was starting to accept his circumstance, move on in a positive way, and keep his emotions in check. But thoughts and realities are often not the same.

CHAPTER TWO

IN A PLACE FAR AWAY

Alta Vista
Costa Rica, 1953

The brilliant, early morning sun broke out over the looming mountainous horizon, casting early dawn light on the dark valley below. Streaks of clouds that eclipsed the tree canopy dispersed, chasing away the remaining gray shadows. The increasing humming sound of propellers swirling nearby filled the canyon with a tremendous roar as a helicopter began its descent into the tiny village of Alta Vista.

The Sisters of Mercy Missionary helicopter was fast approaching, swirling and kicking up dust on its descent.

"It's here. It's here. The helicopter and Doctor Oliver

are here. I can't wait to see her," Ewan told his father as he pointed toward the eastern horizon. His excitement was contagious.

"I saw it, Ewan, coming up over the mountain top," Negos said.

"Doctor Oliver is here!" Ewan exclaimed.

Ewan, Negos, several elder villagers, and other children ran over to the landing spot to greet their bi-weekly visitor and receive their eagerly awaited medicines and treats.

As the chopper landed, Doctor Anale Oliver removed her earmuffs and released her safety harness. She opened the door and waved her hand out to the excited villagers. The pilot turned off the engine to quiet the blades and shut down the instrument panel. He would rest for a few hours and have some food before continuing his deliveries to other remote villages that pocketed the area. The chopper pilot would rendezvous back to pick up the doctor in four days. That was the schedule. As the whirling blades were coming to a stop, Doctor Oliver climbed down the two steps onto the exit platform and into the swirling dust-swept landing spot below her.

"Hello, my friends. It's good to see all of you again. I am happy to be back. I have brought more medicine, food, gifts, and the items you requested from the States."

"*Muchas gracias*, Doctor!" Ewan yelped as he ran up and gave the doctor a big hug around her waist. Then he took the bag of goodies she had for him off her hands.

The Boruca Indians living in Alta Vista were a happy

people. They embraced a simple existence. They called it *pura vida*, the good life, a pure life. They spent their days hunting, gathering, fishing, and farming. The afternoon was for relaxing, taking a break from the heat, visiting, playing, and socializing. The men would go out each morning to hunt, fish, or tend to the crops. The women cared for the young and the elderly; cleaned, washed, and stitched hides; gathered fruits and vegetables, and most importantly, kept the firewood stocked and dry. All was done for the common good of the village. The men cleaned their daily catch or the game they killed, then roasted it over an open fire pit, shared by all who cared to join in. The evenings were full of festive music and dancing: a simple peaceful way that made Dr. Oliver feel at peace.

The small village of Alta Vista sat in a valley that cradled an expansive plateau along a vast mountain range in Costa Rica. So remote and secluded it took four days to hike in or out. It could take more time if carrying a heavy weight or if inclement weather set in, making it more treacherous. There were only three ways in, by foot, on horseback, or by helicopter, which was often the case during rainy season. Many of the people were born, raised, schooled, married, died, and buried in Alta Vista without ever wanting, desiring, or needing to venture outside of the village territory. This was the life of most but not for all.

"*Con mucho gusto,*" Doctor Oliver replied with a big smile, reaching out to hold Ewan's hand as they started walking toward the village center. Doctor Oliver always brought Ewan a six-pack of Coca Cola, which he was inclined to keep for himself.

Many of the other villagers were gathering around them. They were wondering what supplies or other goodies the good doctor brought with her from America.

Doctor Oliver gave Negos an affectionate glance as he strolled beside them, carrying her bags. The three of them continued their walk to the village hospital while the others followed behind in lockstep.

The hospital was a simple four-walled structure with a dirt floor and a gabled palm-frond roof. It was open aired to keep it cool during the humid days. Inside, three beds were lined up against one wall for patients to rest. During her visits, Doctor Oliver would tend to the village people by providing basic medical care and routine checkups, including vaccinations for polio, tuberculosis, typhoid fever, or malaria. She performed minor surgery, set broken bones, stitched up wounds, presided over midwife deliveries, and dispensed pharmaceuticals to rid infection as needed or for pain relief. She even taught them preventive health measures.

Negos was a burly, stout indigenous Indian. He was taller than average with a stocky build and a square chin. His black hair and brown eyes were more dominant than most of his peers. Negos was, as the locals would say: *guapo* (handsome) and *fuerte* (strong), which in his culture would entice women to him in flocks, much like a male frigatebird does while flaunting its red gular to attract female frigates. As for his physical magnetism,

Negos' moral compass was tested on a regular basis; he could have just about any of the women of the village. More importantly, he was a hunter, a provider, and a protector. These were the most valued traits to a woman when selecting a mate, especially when living in the rain forest in a place as remote as Alta Vista, where natural disasters and lurking dangers were part of daily life.

Negos took Marial as his wife when he was fifteen years old. She was the most beautiful girl in the village with her angelic face, long flowing black hair, dark eyes, and perfectly toned and curved body. Marial was also fifteen at the time. Ewan was born a year later.

The people of Alta Vista wanted to make Doctor Oliver feel comfortable, as if the village were her home. She had done so much for them. They catered to her needs and wants as best they could.

After a long day of attending to several patients with cuts and bruises, headaches, and small abrasions, Chief Yanto invited Doctor Oliver to join him, his pregnant wife Sierra, and the elders of the village for dinner. They feasted on a typical Boruca meal of *casado* with rice, gallo beans, black beans, vegetables, and fresh fish. Negos had shot the wild hog with a bow earlier that day. Now it was dressed out in a fancy display. For dessert there was a selection of fresh banana, papaya, and pineapple. The homemade sangria was plentiful for all. The villagers entertained Doctor Oliver with aboriginal dancing and music until late into the evening with spiritual chanting for fire, water, children, and mother earth. The full moon cast a bluish hue of light around them that filled the night with a magical air.

As the night moved along and the campfire slowly burned down, a slight chill emerged. The villagers wrapped themselves with furs as they huddled around the dimming light of the open fire pit.

Suddenly out of the peaceful calm, Sierra cried out in pain.

"Doctor Oliver, it's time. I am going to have my baby." The contraction she felt caused her to roll on her side, holding her belly to her knees. Doctor Oliver came to her aide as did Chief Yanto, Ewan, and his girlfriend, Jemma. Negos, Marial, and the rest of the village elders stood back, looking on.

Doctor Oliver felt Sierra's belly. "Yes, you are, Sierra. Let's get you to your hut."

"Chief Yanto, Negos, help me get Sierra up on her feet. Marial, run ahead to their hut and boil some water," Doctor Scott instructed.

With Negos' help, Chief Yanto raised Sierra up under her arms, cradling her as she hurriedly walked to their hut. Ewan and Doctor Oliver were one step ahead. As they reached the hut, Doctor Oliver pushed open the door.

"Lay her on her side on the bed. Make her comfortable. I need to get some clean sheets. Marial, bring me the hot water."

Chief Yanto placed his wife on the bed, tenderly holding her hand but with the tightest of grips.

"I am here for you, my wife. Soon you will have our baby," Chief Yanto proclaimed, not wanting to let go.

"Now the three of you leave us be. I will take it from here," Doctor Oliver instructed as she brought over a bucket of water and some towels to Sierra's bedside.

Sierra gave his hand a tender squeeze with hers as if to tell him everything would be fine. Chief Yanto released his hand slowly.

Once Doctor Oliver and Sierra were alone, she examined Sierra. "You are dilated to eight centimeters already. I can see the head. When you feel the urge to push, take deep breaths and push hard."

Not a minute later, Sierra began to push. "Take a deep breath and push again, like this," Doctor Oliver said as she mimicked the breathing technique.

Sierra did as she was told. She pushed and took a deep breath as instructed. The pain was agonizing. Sierra clenched her teeth, squeezing her fists hard to suppress the pain.

With Doctor Oliver's encouragement, now determined more than ever to end this, Sierra pushed harder. The baby's head was fully exposed when Doctor Oliver reached in tenderly around the baby's neck and shoulders, pulling the baby girl out slowly and gently. When the baby did not cry, Doctor Oliver spanked the baby to get her to start breathing on her own. The baby started wailing loudly. Sierra relaxed with a big sigh. She had just given birth to their little princess. Doctor Oliver cut the umbilical cord, cleaned the sticky white vernix off the baby girl, and wrapped her in a woolen blanket. She then happily handed over the bundle of joy to Sierra.

"You have a baby girl, Chief Yanto," Doctor Oliver called out to him through the door. Ewan heard her from outside the dirt walls, as well as did several other villagers who arrived to witness the birth.

"It's a baby girl," Ewan yelled out in his excitement.

The baby weighted seven pounds, five ounces. She was nineteen inches long with thick, curly, jet black hair. And she had the lungs of an opera singer.

"I will name her Suneda, a name as beautiful as this sunrise will be today," Chief Yanto proclaimed proudly as he walked out to where the excited villagers were gathered, cradling his daughter. Holding her small body cupped in his hands, he raised her up to the sky.

"This is Princess Suneda," Chief Yanto said as he raised baby Suneda high above his head.

The villagers started singing and clapping their hands together, praying and chanting to Sibo. Suneda was the first girl born in the village in several years.

"Princess Suneda, Princess Suneda, may Sibo bless our Princess Suneda and bring us all good fortune," Chief Yanto prayed.

Chief Yanto brought the baby back inside and laid her on her mother's lap. He hugged his wife and thanked her for their beautiful child. He was so happy. Yanto was a proud chief and father of a princess.

Doctor Oliver was exhausted from the long night. She examined Sierra one last time before heading back to her own hut as the early dawn light was beginning to creep up over the horizon.

Negos was inside waiting for her. Two years earlier, in a moment of weakness, Negos began a love affair with Doctor Oliver. He was curious about her. He loved the way she cared for the villagers. He loved her smile. Her laughter and humor were contagious. Doctor Oliver was an average looking woman, but every time they embraced, the blueness in her eyes drew him in. Maybe it was because she was different than the women in his village. He had heard many stories about these beautiful white women while growing up. Negos looked forward to her visits each and every month. He longed for her touch, the sweet smell of her skin that engulfed his senses and teased his raw animalist instinct, taking control of his thinking. Once this took over, he could not shake her scent. He didn't want to. He thought about her all the time, wanting to be with her always. They made love every chance they could. He believed she loved him too.

Doctor Oliver was curious about Negos too. He was attractive, smart, and strong. He had an air of confidence about him that she never felt with any other man. It was not arrogance; rather, he was a man's man, a simple jungle man who was completely comfortable with who he was. These qualities were pleasing to her.

Doctor Oliver could not get enough of his love, yearning for his tenderness when they were apart. Negos was the man she had always dreamed of, and thoughts of him consumed her heart. She looked forward to her trips back to Alta Vista so she could be held in his big, strong arms again.

They loved each other, even knowing what they were doing was wrong. A path destined for self-destruction. Over time, Doctor Oliver's guilty conscious was consuming her moral compass. She felt it had to stop. It was only a matter of time.

Doctor Oliver motioned Negos to come sit down next to her on the bed.

"My sweet Anale, I have missed you so," Negos said as he sat down and placed his arm around her.

"And I have missed you, my dear Negos," Doctor Oliver replied with sadness in her voice.

She turned toward him and firmly wrapped her arms around him. Holding back tears, she squeezed him tenderly. Negos held her closely with his strong arms. He kissed her passionately on her soft, welcoming lips, then worked his way along the side of her neck. The floral aroma of her skin captivated his senses. She was right there and he was ready for her. Anale cupped the back of Negos head with her hands as he began unbuttoning and slipping off her dress. The garment fell down to her hips. Negos pulled her to standing and the dress fell around her feet. He gently picked her up and lowered her to the bed. He slid off her panties, then took off his pants and underwear. He lay down beside her. Anale turned over to look into his loving, dark brown eyes and then kissed his hairy chest. She rubbed her breasts on his. Her touch was beyond his control now. It was time to feel all of her, for her to feel all of him inside of her. He rolled her over and moved on top of her. She was ready for him.

"Slowly, Negos, let's take it slow this time," Anale whispered in his ear. She closed her eyes, the thought of their pleasure was more than she could bear. She knew in her heart this would be the last time. It had to be.

"I love you, Anale," Negos told her as he positioned himself over her.

"I know you do, my sweet man, as you know I love you." He could feel her warm and moist as he entered deep inside her, slowly at first as she had commanded and then at a more fast, rhythmic pace. The sounds of her subtle moaning made him large and thick. They embraced each other as though they were one, moving together, feeling each other, knowing each other. Her smooth and ample breasts pressed against him and he could no longer hold back his desire as he readied to release himself inside her.

She could feel him, truly feel him; her jungle man stiffening and swelling, filling her up to the point of release. Wildly unabated, their orgasmic pleasure was more intense than ever before. Their two hearts beat frantically, pumped joyfully, as they separated from one another. Their breathing was heavy as they tried to catch their breath. Lying flat on their backs looking up to the heavens, they searched for a future where none existed.

"Negos, you know I love you with all my heart and soul but this has to stop. This is not right. You are a married man. You have a wife, a child to care for, a son to follow you."

"We can make it work, Anale. I will leave with you. We can start a new beginning in America," Negos pleaded.

"I will not let you destroy your family, your way of life over me. I could not. We could not live with the guilt and hurt. It will not work. It simply won't work," Anale said firmly.

Deep in his being Negos knew she was right. He realized this moment would come someday but hoped it would not be this soon. It was getting light outside. It was time for Negos to leave. Doctor Oliver turned away as Negos got up and walked toward the door.

Marial rolled over in bed, reaching out for Negos. Adjusting her eyes in the dark to see as her hand reached a space that was empty and cold. Searching through the sheets, denying that once again Negos was not there as he had not been many nights before when Doctor Oliver visited. Angry and hurt, Marial got up from bed and got dressed, this time determined to confront the truth. She stomped heavy-footed over to Doctor Oliver's hut to prove her instinct was correct. As she approached Doctor Oliver's, Negos was just leaving. He looked up and saw Marial coming.

"Negos, how could you do this to us, with Doctor Oliver? You are my husband, my man. We have a child. You have destroyed our family," Marial cried out, running up to Negos. He turned and started to walk away, head down, looking at the ground. Marial jumped on Negos back. She scratched and clawed at the back of his neck, hissing and screaming. Negos pushed her off and turned around. Marial slapped him as hard as she could and then dropped to her knees crying.

"Why did you do this, Negos, why?"

Negos had nothing to say. He was lost in thought, searching for an answer.

"Why did you do this, Anale, why?"

Doctor Oliver listened from inside her hut, feeling ashamed. Most of the village heard the commotion too. They knew what had been going on.

"Our poor, sweet Marial, how could Negos and Doctor Oliver do this to her?" The hush of the gossiping villagers was as loud as ever.

CHAPTER THREE

STICKS AND STONES

The Youth Village Detention Center
Huntsville, Texas, 1972

"You can have this hothead case, doctor, we are done with the troublemaker for now," the taller of the two guards told Dr. Scott as he pushed Billie down to sit in the chair across from her.

"Thank you, Officer Potts," Doctor Scott replied.

"We'll be right outside the door if you need us," Officer Potts said. The two men exited the room and closed the door behind them.

Billie had just turned twenty years old, and he was facing another five years confinement, this time at the

Huntsville State Prison, for busting the nose of a fellow inmate by the name of Bobby Ward. Billie had grown to be a strikingly handsome young man with baby blue eyes as mesmerizing as a New Mexico sky. Billie was a head turner, standing over six feet two inches tall. His body was muscular, bouncing-quarter hard from working out daily in his cell. The V-shaped build he crafted came out of his aggressions. He was physically strong, mentally tough, and ready to defend himself anywhere and at any time.

Billie was shackled at the ankles with handcuffs around his wrists, wearing an orange jump suit as he sat, eyes down, across from the doctor.

"Billie, tell me about this Bobby Ward. What happened today? I can't help you get out of here if these outbursts of anger and assault continue," Doctor Scott pleaded with him.

"You really want to know? You want to know how it went down," Billie questioned in a huff.

"Yes, tell me everything. What happened?"

"Okay doc. We were just playing a friendly game of pool and he said, 'Billie boy, are you going to take the shot or just play with yourself and that little stick of yours?'" Billie told her in his best Bobby Ward imitation.

"Go ahead, Billie, I am listening."

"That piece of shit Ward was teasing me, trying to rush me and distract me from the winning shot."

"I see, so what happened next?"

"I stood up to walk around to the other side of the

table, sizing up my shot for the win...." Billie hesitated. "I can't stand that fucker," he said excitedly.

"Was that it? That's all he said? You beat him up for that? These anger fits and outbursts have got to stop," Doctor Scott implored.

"No, that's not what set me off. It's too late anyway. What difference does it make?"

"So what was it? What triggered the outburst, Billie?" Doctor Scott probed, trying to get to the bottom of his anger pit once and for all. Billie hesitated for a moment before speaking, his head down, focusing on the terrazzo flooring.

"Then he said, 'Hey there, lover boy, have you been on all fours lately? I heard your papa made you oink like a little pig,' that's what the porker said."

"What did you say to him when he questioned your manhood like that?"

" 'What did you say, asshole?' is what I said."

"And that was it?" Dr. Scott asked.

"No. Then he started making pig sounds. 'Oink... Oink...Whee...Whee...' " Billie said, mimicking Bobby Ward's voice.

Doctor Scott rubbed her forehead. "I see, then what did you do?"

"I looked directly at his sorry fat ass, caulked the stick, then cracked him right upside his fuckin', brain-less head.

"Oh, my God, Billie." Doctor Scott sat back hard in

her chair as if he had hit her as well. It took her a moment to respond. "How did that make you feel?"

"Are you serious doctor? It made me feel good. The sound of hickory and bone crushing in sync, mangling together against that fucker's face was pure joy to my ears; it was musical. Bobby Ward had been bullying me and others in the ward way too long. I simply took justice in my hand, enough was enough. Now he looks like the son of Jimmy Durante. Bobby Durante…ha…ha…Yes, that's it, baby Bobby Durante," Billie chuckled.

"Jesus, Billie."

"I cracked him a couple more times on the top of his noggin to make sure he wouldn't get up. Then the guards grabbed me and dragged me by my feet to solitaire to put me in these restraints.

"I can understand how that could make you angry, Billie. He was being a bully, but you can't continue to fight over the past, surely not to beat someone over it. You need to move forward with your life," Doctor Scott said, exasperation in her voice.

"I know doc. It eats at me. Certain things set me off. I can't control it. I am trying. He did deserve it, though," Billie said solemnly.

"I'll see what I can do, Billie. The court will allow me the courtesy to write up a disposition on your mental state before sentencing. Maybe the Judge will be lenient. At least I can ask him to let us continue our sessions. He should agree to that. When is your day in court?"

"In a couple of weeks. I'll be in solitaire until then, me and my orange creamsicle suit."

Doctor Scott instructed Officer Potts to come in and take Billie back to his cell.

As she watched Billie shuffle and clank his way down the hall, she thought about what usually happened to men in the state penitentiary. It usually wasn't good.

CHAPTER FOUR

THE HUNT FOR TAPIR

A few days after Doctor Oliver delivered Suneda, she left and never came back. The helicopter took her away, crying and remorseful for what she had done. Whisking her away in an instant from Negos' memory as the sounds of the blades sank over the horizon. He watched from afar as she left, upset and ashamed, never to hold her or kiss her again or to say his last goodbye to his sweet Doctor Oliver.

Six months went by and he wondered why she never returned to him. Why had she told him she loved him then abandoned him, leaving him out in the cold? He often hoped she would come on the next flight, the next trip, but it was never the case; the monthly supplies and medicines would arrive by other doctors, missionaries, and traders. Not one of them would tell him what happened to her. Not one of them seemed to care or know anything about her.

Negos almost lost Marial because of his adulterous ways. Negos admitted his mistake and asked for her forgiveness. He pleaded with her and promised never to seek the comforts of another woman. Having another woman in his life was not meant to be, he understood this, even though he was heartbroken. He had to move on with his life.

He did. They both did, then Negos lost his wife two years later, during the birth of their second son. Without the proper medical care afforded developed countries, losing a child at birth was not uncommon in Alta Vista, but Negos blamed himself for their death. He believed Sibo took Marial and his unborn son as punishment for his unholy ways. He begged Sibo to release him from his tormented soul, but it seemed he wasn't listening.

Her death took a great toll on the rest of Marial's family too. Sierra, Marial's sister, knew of the "missionary sin" as did many of the villagers, who also held Negos responsible for Marial's death. Suneda did not know what was going on between her mother and her uncle, she was too young at the time. And by the time she was old enough to understand, no one would talk about it. Even if she did, it would not have mattered to her anyway. The missionary woman brought her into this life. Besides, Negos was her uncle, friend, and confidante.

The mistakes Negos made weighed heavily on his mental state. It was one cross in life he would have to bear.

Ewan missed Doctor Oliver too. "Father, why has Doctor Oliver abandoned us? She left us without saying goodbye. I don't understand," Ewan would ask Negos time and time again.

Negos had no answer, only lies. "I do not know," Negos said abruptly.

"I miss her so much," Ewan said.

"I miss her too, my son. I pray she is safe and that she will return to us someday."

+

Eight years had passed and no word ever came of Doctor Oliver. Negos and Ewan seldom brought up her name, although both of them thought about her often.

Negos went about his life as a single father, raising and teaching Ewan in the customary Boruca ways. He taught Ewan how to swim, track, build tools, make spears, tie knots, create fire, fish, and hunt when he was very young. At fifteen Ewan was becoming the man that any father would be proud of. He was a marksman with a bow and arrow, hitting a coati—a small raccoon-like animal— running at full speed when others missed by a meter. During tribal contests, Ewan could split an arrow from fifty meters. Many times he would bring home a wild boar all on his own. The apple of his father's eye had gained the respect of the other men in the village. He was very strong and bright, just like his father. Negos envisioned Ewan as a leader of his people someday, perhaps the next chief. Ewan was a tall muscular young man. He had curly, dark brown hair like his mother Marial had that flowed down past his neck line. Big brown eyes and a straight jaw line were clear enough evidence that Ewan was Negos' son. There was no mistake about it.

On a misty, fall morning, before dawn, Negos entered Ewan's bedroom to wake him for the annual tapir hunt. The jungle pig was a staple of the village for its meat and its hide. It was this time of year the tapir would migrate north during the heavy rainy season into the mountainous regions to forage for food. The Boruca would hunt them down for winter sustenance. Groups of four or six would encircle a pack of tapir. As the circle closed in on the animals, the hunters would bang sticks loudly, howling and grunting to confuse the animals, getting them to scatter in all directions. As the tapir leaped to avoid capture, the hunters would raise their spears and lance the beasts and fell them on the spot.

The village hunters were to meet in the village center at daybreak.

"Wake up, Ewan, the tapir will be gathering in the valley this morning. We need to meet up with the others," Negos said. He shook him by his shoulder to get him up and going.

"Yes, father, I am ready," Ewan said with a yawn. Stretching out his arms, shaking away the sleep, Ewan rose and quickly followed his father, his spear in hand.

Six hunters were waiting, ready to go. They marched off in single file. Negos and Ewan took up the rear position.

Negos and Ewan went off together, stalking a pair of tapir that moved into a densely forested area far away from the other hunters. The rain began to fall, starting as a drizzle, to a steady downpour, then becoming torrential buckets in short order. Visibility was no more than one or two meters. They had the two tapir cornered up against a steep embankment and were slowly closing in on them. They began howling and banging their sticks. Before they threw their spears, the smaller one slipped past them both as it leaped over a large boulder that separated them. The remaining tapir, the bigger one, made its move in desperation. Charging at them head first, it jumped as high as it could. Negos and Ewan jabbed their spears simultaneously into the tapir's underbelly piercing skin, muscle, and tissue as it flew between them. With a howl and then an unforgettable scream, the tapir began kicking and rolling around on the muddy ground, trying to regain footing. Ewan stood still, Negos' spear lodged deep within his chest. He looked up at his father in confusion, then fell.

Negos looked at the tapir, then over to Ewan, unsure as to what just happened. He wiped the rain water from his eyes in disbelief.

Negos dropped to his knees next to Ewan. "My son, my son, oh my God, what have I done to my son?" Negos cried out in deep despair, looking to the heavens, a cry so highly pitched it seemed to stop the beating down rain for just a moment. Negos took his son's lifeless body in his arms "Ewan, please wake up my son. I need you here with me."

Ewan made no sound.

Negos tried for hours to revive his son. Holding him and rocking him close to his heart until he finally had to accept that Ewan was dead. Negos laid his son down under a banyan tree. He prayed to Sibo for Ewan's soul and to be delivered from his own unjust life. He was being punished, again.

Negos buried Ewan that day. He prayed to Sibo for forgiveness.

What would he tell the villagers? He was Negos, the great provider and protector, the fearless hunter. Not willing or daring to tell the truth, he wanted to bury this unforgettable tragedy in a deep crater somewhere in the back of his mind.

When he returned, Negos told the villagers that he and Ewan were heading back to the village from the hunt because of the heavy rains. While crossing the bridge to Alta Vista, at Big Fork, Ewan stumbled on a knot protruding from the warping boards. He slipped and fell into the raging Baru River and was swept up violently in the current, taken way downstream beyond his site.

Not given up for dead, several villagers, led by Negos, traversed the riverbanks for days, tracking for miles downstream in search of Ewan's body after the flooding water subsided.

After months of lies and deceit, Negos could no

longer stand to live with himself, let alone face the people who believed in him. Who had he become? His longing to leave the village and strike out on his own, to start a new life, a fresh beginning, beckoned him. As the weeks went by, the yearnings became more intense. Negos knew it was time for him to leave Alta Vista. He had no other choice; withdrawal was the only answer that made any sense: leave the past behind or live here in agony for what he had done and what he had failed to do.

The morning Negos left, he packed lightly for the dangerous, four-day trek in the mountainous terrain to the coastal town of Puerto Viejo on the Caribbean coast. The sun would soon break over the high peaks, shedding the light of a new day on the village. It was time to leave. Negos picked up his bag and walked to Suneda's bedroom window.

"Psst…psst, Suneda, wake up. It's me, Negos. I wanted to say goodbye to you before I leave," Negos whispered to her through her open window.

Suneda woke and rubbed her eyes to gain focus. She stood and quietly went to her window to look out.

"What? Why are you leaving, Uncle? You can't leave, I will miss you too much."

"I can't face my past here any longer. It is too painful. From losing my Marial and the baby and now Ewan, how can I stay here any longer?" Negos said with a heavy sadness in his voice.

"Where will you go? What will you do?"

"You and I have talked about this many times. You

want to become a doctor as much as I long to be out at sea, in the open ocean, free to breathe fresh air," Negos said with a sigh.

"Suneda, the sea is calling my name. It is my path. I will find work at the Port of Viejo and sail throughout the Caribbean and the Gulf of Mexico. I will travel out of the Port of Limon, to Belize, Honduras, Houston, Beaumont, New Orleans, Caymans, and Rotan. My journey will set me free from the ghosts of my past, to shake them from my haunted existence and start a new future, one with the sea. Sibo will forgive me. This is what I must do to save my soul. You will take your chosen path as well someday, my beautiful Suneda. I have seen the sadness in your eyes, the boredom in your efforts, resisting the wishes of your father and your mother. You need for more than what Alta Vista can give you. At sixteen you are old enough to make your own mark on this world. Do what you must do before it is too late. Rather than say goodbye, we will see each other again, this I promise you," Negos said as he picked up his pack, turned his back to Suneda and walked off.

+

Suneda was devastated when Negos left. Although she understood his need to search for a different life, the depression felt from being left behind was an enormous strain on her.

"Follow your path. It is yours to take. No one else

can follow it for you. The one you choose will become your destiny just like your grandfather did." Suneda would repeat this in her mind, convincing herself that Negos was right.

Suneda knew she wanted to become a doctor, just like the missionaries who flew into Alta Vista every month to deliver medicine and medical care to the locals, just like Doctor Oliver used to do. The missionaries tutored Suneda in English and told her stories about life in America. The world they described to her was so different from her life in the village. She wanted to experience that life on her own. Suneda focused on her study of the English language, becoming bilingual by the time she was ten years old.

Suneda preferred studying medical books in English over playing with the other children in the village. The daily lecturing and bitter nagging from her mother and father to learn the woman-ways of the village were driving her crazy. They would not listen or even consider her wishes. She had had enough of the constant badgering of her parents, trying to change her way of thinking. Suneda took the advice Negos gave her a few weeks earlier and struck out to fulfill her own dream. She ran away, stowed away under some blankets piled in the cargo hold of the medical supply transport helicopter.

Hiding quietly in the hold area, she was determined to pursue the American dream she'd heard so much about. This was her path, her destiny. No one would stop her from becoming a doctor.

When Suneda did not show up for dinner that night, her family thought she fell to her death, just like they believed Ewan had, on the bridge that lead into or out of Alta Vista. It was raining hard the day Suneda disappeared, making the bridge treacherous for crossing. It was not uncommon for one or two villagers to fall to their death every year. It was old, worn out, and missing some of its wooden slats. Sections of the rope were missing and rotted, overexposed to the elements. In addition, patches of wet, green, slimy moss spread across the teak foot boards and amplified its dangerous condition for anyone attempting to cross. People simply got swept away downstream by the raging river below, never to be found or heard of again.

Chief Yanto, Sierra, and all the other villagers were devastated when they thought they lost Suneda to the raging river. They held a funeral procession with a wooden casket feathered with banana leaves, lined with pink hibiscus, and scented with white gardenias. It was a day of mourning and of celebration, knowing, believing that Suneda was to be in the comfort of Sibo's great hands.

It didn't take long for Suneda to wish she were dead.

CHAPTER
FIVE

JAKE THE MONSTER

Houston, Texas, 1956

Billie, Elana, and Jake were on their way to a birthday party for little Billie at Rainbow Palace, the local ice cream parlor, when Jake abruptly pulled over to the side of the road and stopped the car.

"I know what you are up to, Elana. You've been planning to run off with my Billie," Jake said.

"What are you talking about?" Elana said trembling.

"I overheard you talking to that bitch sister of yours," Jake shot back. "She's gonna pick you and Billie up at the party and head to Oklahoma. You've been planning this for a long time, haven't you? I read the letter you sent her." He got out of the car and opened the trunk, taking something out before slamming it shut.

"He is my Billie, not yours, Jake. I gave birth to him. You're not his real father. You have hurt him, me, and us. Enough is enough. I can't take this anymore. You are not a man, you are a monster," she said with fear in her voice.

Elana met Jake Jensen when she came home to the States with Billie when he was a one-year-old. She was living in a small one-bedroom apartment on the south side of Houston, across from Lincoln Park. Jake operated a mobile ice cream truck near the park. Every day Billie and Elana took a morning stroll through the park, stopping to enjoy the slides and swings with an occasional ice cream cone from Jake's truck. Usually, only small talk occurred between Elana and Jake when he served them.

One day, as Billie was climbing up the yellow slide, he slipped and fell. Jake happened to be sitting on a bench close by, watching them. He came to the rescue, catching Billie just as he hit the ground. Elana came rushing over to help Billie too. Jake talked to Billie like a father, bouncing him on his knee, talking to him in a soft, comforting voice; he was a charmer. Billie instantly felt safe with him. He stopped crying as Jake brushed the woodchip debris from his shirt and pants. Billie took Jake's hand, leading him to the swings, pointing out the one he wanted to sit on. Jake hoisted him up to sit on the special swing Billie picked out and proceeded to push him back and forth. Billie was laughing and giggling. Elana smiled at the tall, attractive man. They talked that day for hours, filling a void Elana didn't even realize even existed in her life. Jake seemed to come to rescue her too.

Jake wined and dined Elana and Billie for three months. It was always the three of them together, family time, quality time, bonding them. They married after a short engagement. She quit working and changed her name to Elana Jensen, glad to drop the stigma of being a single mother without a husband. Jake charmed her into thinking he would be good a father figure, but time proved otherwise. Jake slowly turned controlling, threatening to hurt her or Billie, though he never did. Elana knew that it would be just a matter of time, so she had made plans to leave him and take Billie with her.

Elana was holding Billie tightly, locking him against her chest while rocking him back and forth, trying to keep him from getting upset. When Jake opened her side door, he pulled Billie from her grasp, tossing him to the ground, unconcerned for his safety as he started crying and reaching back for his mother.

"Jake, what are you doing? You're hurting me," Elana whimpered, begging him to let her go as he started to drag her out of the car. "Stop it. Please stop," Fighting to stay in the vehicle, flailing with her free arm to grab onto anything, she landed on his face and used her nails to scratch deeply into his cheek.

Jake screeched out in pain. Reactively, he punched her as hard as he could with a clenched fist, knocking her silly. In a last-ditch effort, Elana wedged her foot under the passenger seat in a futile attempt to keep herself from being removed. She knew she was in trouble, in fear for their lives. It was too late. Jake pulled her from the car and began to pummel her head with the crowbar he took out from the trunk of the car.

Too young to understand why his father was hitting his mother, Billie put his thumb in his mouth and sucked it. He wet his pants. He covered his eyes with his tiny hands, not really knowing what was happening.

"Daddy, Daddy, Mommy, Mommy, go home now?" Billie cried out.

"You're going to kill me," Elana screamed as she tried to cover her head with her arms to deflect the rusty iron bar.

Jake proceeded to hit her several more times. Elana, no longer able to fight him off, gave in to unconsciousness as the lights went out.

"That should do it. You are not taking Billie from me, you little bitch," Jake shouted as he discarded the tire iron into a grassy knoll next to her body. He picked Billie up and gave him a suffocating hug, then kissed Billie on his lips.

"You are my boy, Billie," Jake said as he buckled Billie into the front seat next to him.

"Daddy, we go home now. Mommy, Mommy come back. Daddy some ice cream now," Billie said as he looked out the window, befuddled at his mother lying outside on the ground next to the car.

"Shut up," Jake said to Billie.

Nothing else was said during that lonely isolated

drive to a trailer park across town. Exhausted, Billie fell asleep with his thumb in his mouth, tear streaks on his cheeks.

Elana was lying face down in the ditch where Jake left her with a broken jaw and multiple contusions and abrasions across most of her back, arms, and sides.

Several hours later, a young woman found her limp, lifeless body. It was raining heavily that afternoon. The ditch had filled with six inches of water. A few more hours and Elana would have drowned in the muddy culvert. She woke a few days later only to realize, to acknowledge, to no longer deny that Jake had taken off with her Billie.

"Where is my Billie?" Elana screamed out loud, frantically searching for answers.

"Calm down miss. You need to settle down before you hurt yourself," one of the hospital nurses told her.

"Calm down! What do you mean calm down. I need to find my Billie right now!" Elana yelled.

"We know nothing of your Billie, ma'am. You were found with hardly a pulse, almost dead off Interstate 35, north of Wichita Falls. You were the only person there, according to the young woman who brought you here. Can you tell us what happened?" the nurse asked.

"I was trying to escape to safety with my little boy when the monster took him from me. He did this to me. He took my Billie."

"Who did this to you, miss? What monster are you referring too? Who took Billie?"

"Jake Jensen, his stepfather. You have to find them

before he hurts my Billie!" Elana screamed loudly at the nurse as Elana tried to get out of the bed. A larger nurse came into the room and came toward Elana, tapping a syringe.

"What are you doing? You have no right to do this! Don't you dare stick that fucking needle in my arm," Elana yelled as the big nurse proceeded to hold her down and stick the needle firmly into her right shoulder.

"This will calm you down, Mrs. Jensen. It will help you sleep," the nurse said calmly as she dispensed the sedative into Elana's arm.

"I don't want to sleep. I have to save my Billie. And don't call me Mrs. Jensen. I am not her anymore. I don't want to be her anymore," Elana insisted as she tried to pull away. A few moments later she was sound asleep, drifting off to another world, safe from her hell on earth.

During her stay Elana was given heavy doses of valium to keep her under control and to protect her from herself. The agony, suffering, and guilt were unbearable. Eventually Elana had a nervous breakdown and was placed in a mental hospital. She remained institutionalized for two years, until she could control herself and function back in society.

CHAPTER SIX

SUNNY ON THE STREETS

Harris County Court House
Houston, Texas, 1972

Suneda walked into the hallway outside the courtroom while being closely guarded by a plump female security guard. She was waiting for her arraignment and a court-appointed attorney to escort her in.

"Hey, you okay?" Billie asked her. He was sitting in shackles and cuffs on a bench just across from where she was standing.

"Are you talking...talking...to me?" Suneda said, coughing. She coughed so hard she had to lean up against the wall for support. "Please just leave me alone. I don't feel very well," Suneda said, then she began to cry.

Billie got up as quickly as his restraints would allow and walked over to catch her from falling. Billie's guard moved toward him, but when he saw what he was doing, he relaxed back up against the wall.

Billie held Suneda's hand tightly, squeezing it to comfort her. He wondered about the unexplained sensations he was feeling from his close proximity to the most gorgeous woman he had ever met. She was stunningly beautiful, with long, wavy jet-black hair, flawless exotic facial features, full lips, firm breasts, and nice legs that joined themselves invitingly to well-curved hips. Billie didn't seem to see the dark circles under her red-rimmed eyes.

Suneda's guard immediately pointed to the bench a few feet away. Billie helped Suneda sit, then asked the guard for a Kleenex. She pulled a small, wrapped package out of her pocket and handed it to Billie. Billie gave it to Suneda and sat tentatively next to her. Suneda blew her nose and smiled up at him. Then she surprised Billie by resting her head on his shoulder. Billie stiffened at first, but when she leaned into him, he relaxed, noticing the calm the girl seemed to instantly create just by being near him.

"What's your name?" Billie asked.

"Suneda Ortega. They call me Sunny on the streets," Suneda stated proudly.

"Suneda. What a beautiful name. I am Billie Jensen. It's nice to meet you Sunny-On-The-Streets."

Suneda laughed. It was just the reaction Billie had hoped for.

"I like Suneda. Can I call you Suneda?" Billie asked sincerely.

"Sure, Billie Jensen, it's nice to meet you too." Suneda closed her eyes and then reopened them, looking up to Billie. Her brown eyes locked onto Billie's baby blues.

"Why are you here?" she asked groggily, trying to focus on the conversation. You must have done something pretty bad," she said, looking down at his restraints.

"I busted a guy's nose for calling me names."

"What'd he say?" Suneda asked, surprised.

"It's a long story. All I know is they're going to send me up to the big pen in Huntsville for five more years," Billie said.

"So you have anger issues?"

"No, not really…well, yeah, I guess so. I am working on it. How about you? What's your story?"

"They arrested me for drug possession with intent to distribute. I am here for a deportation hearing."

"Looks like you forgot to distribute," Billie said sarcastically.

"My life has been hell for the last two years, Billie. You have no idea." Suneda sat up and cupped her face in her hands.

"I am sorry, Suneda. I'm an insensitive jerk. Like I said, I am working on some issues, very big issues."

"I just want to go home, Billie."

"Where's your home?"

"My home is in the mountains of Costa Rica, in a village called Alta Vista. It's the most beautiful, peaceful place in the world," Suneda said.

"If it's so damn beautiful and peaceful, why the hell did you come here?" Billie asked.

"I wanted to become a doctor. I wanted the American dream, but I got mixed up in some bad stuff. I guess you could say, I got on the wrong path."

"Yeah, I know how that goes. Sometimes life really stinks. Sometimes you have no choice but to walk the path you're given and make the most of it. I never had a chance to make my own path. It was decided for me, but I plan to change that someday, someday soon," Billie said.

"What is your plan, Billie?" Suneda asked.

Before he could answer, two guards ordered Billie to stand up and walk with them. It was time for him to go to Huntsville.

"Take care of yourself, Suneda. Come see me in Huntsville. We'll talk about our plans," Billie said, hoping she would take him up on his invitation but not expecting her to.

"I just may do that, sweet Billie," Suneda said, then she gave him the most amazing smile he had ever seen.

Billie had an odd tingling feeling deep within himself. "I sure hope you do, beautiful Suneda. Remember, it's Billie Jensen," he said with a smile.

Suneda smiled back as Billie was escorted away.

✦

Suneda never showed up at the Immigration Customs Enforcement deportation station as ordered. Instead she went into hiding, like most deportees did. The courts and ICE rarely give a rat's-ass. They gave you a deportation date, shook you lose, and left it to you to honor it on your own. Suneda actually wanted to go home, but after she had met Billie, she was having second thoughts, good thoughts.

CHAPTER SEVEN

EL SANGUINIO

Huntsville State Prison
Huntsville, Texas

After stretching and adjusting his eyes to the first hint of daylight reflecting off the cold steel bars, Billie dropped to the gritty cell floor. He fought through one hundred pushups: fifty with his right arm, then fifty with his left. When he stood, he became nauseated from the rush. He took in a full breath to fill up his lungs, and then out to avoid puking. Relaxing for a moment, wiping sweat beads off his forehead, he mentally prepared himself for the next round of painful, self-inflicted exercise; he did two hundred and fifty sit-ups followed by two hundred leg squats. Billie's body felt the heat as he reached high above to stretch out his stressed abdominal and thigh muscles, grabbing hold of the cross bar in his empty, sterile cell. He completed the seventy-five chin-ups necessary to finish the routine. With quads and biceps bulging in rock-tight formation, he repeated this exercise routine twice a day, every day. After so many years, it was obvious the daily regimen paid off. His body, chiseled like a Roman statue, was almost God-like.

He shaved, brushed his teeth, took a shit, showered, and dressed. He thought about how today would be different. No life existed here, only dreams, bad dreams. His only motivation for the day was to survive and fulfill his plan. Something had changed deep down within himself after he met Suneda and it gave him a sense of empowerment. It was time to move on, to discard his lowly life.

"It's up to me to make it happen. Failure, no way; it's not an option." He looked at himself in the mirror and reflected on his tormented life. He pondered every step, every minute detail, every moment forward, smiling as he buttoned the last eyehole on his shirt. Then he heard the sound of rattling keys approaching. A couple of cockroaches scurried away as he turned around and walked to the front of his cell. Pete promptly opened his cell door and directed him and several other inmates from his cellblock toward the cafeteria.

"Her comin' up to see me today, that sweet little

honey of ours?" Pete asked while sporting a full-toothed, shit-eating grin.

"Yeah, she's coming today, Pete. Are you going to give us our private time, like we agreed, you piece of shit, or are you going to make me beg?" Billie responded in a huff of discontent. Pete always got Billie's blood pressure boiling, especially when it pertained to his intimate life with the love of his life, his soul mate, his salvation: Suneda.

"I can hardly wait to see her! She's such a beautiful piece of ass. The body and look of a Goddess, I must say. It blows my mind what the hell she sees in a dead-end convict like you, Billie boy," he said, shaking his head. "You know the deal." Pete emphasized his point with a double wink as he scratched his head and turned, walking like a rooster behind him.

Getting Billie's ire up was pure joy for Pete. It gave him a sense of power. For a lowlife security guard he knew he could make life here torturous for Billie, which he did often, merely to stroke his own ego.

Billie's fists clenched in pure rage and his face tightened as he thought about his deal with Pete.

"Easy, Billie; you get what you want and I get what I want. It's that simple, understand me, my man? Now move along, big fella." Pete said. He poked the nightstick up against Billie's ass to prod him along.

Billie knew he needed to keep his composure, especially today. He turned and gave Pete a fake smile. Pete looked at him oddly, knowing Billie couldn't stand the sight of him. Unfortunately for Billie, though, Pete was his "handler," which meant he was in charge of his every move. Nothing was fair about it; it was just a fact. Billie imagined himself grabbing the nightstick and shoving it way up into Pete's scrawny ass.

"What the hell are you smiling for, Billie boy?"

"Nothing at all, Pete, you sick fucking peeper," Billie spit back.

Pete blew Billie's attitude off with a flick of his wrist, then proceeded to swing his eighteen-inch nightstick back and forth to shuttle the rest of them along like a herd of cattle. Pete was always prepared for a fight or at least to defend himself if necessary. He was a stocky fellow with well-defined biceps. He lifted weights on a regular basis. Billie thought of him as a perverted meathead type with a small dick, someone who could only get his jollies off watching other people screwing. A sick fuck. A dick, really, in Billie's mind.

He did have to be aware of his surroundings though. After all, if walking in his shoes, readiness was a must. The inmates here were a cesspool mixture of murders, serial killers, rapists, and thugs, quite a few notches more serious than the kids at the juvenile correctional facility. Some were humans, some were nonhumans, and a good share of them were subhuman. Any one of them at any time would slit another inmate's throat just for giving them an odd look or for saying something they didn't like.

Fights would break out just to relieve the boredom. Everyone took sides, some for protection, some for fun, but most did it to survive another day. If someone got hurt, they were sent directly to the infirmary for medical attention. A change of scenery from the dark, dank, gray cellblocks was almost always welcomed by this sorry bunch of no-good losers. To break up any shuffles, Pete enjoyed cracking them upside their heads with his hard, oak nightstick. He knew that this place was home for most of them for the rest of their lives, so it was his way of showing all of them who was the boss of the house.

Mostly, though, the inmates were consumed with fear. But they would not, could not, no way in hell could they ever show it. Showing weakness of any kind was not in their best interest.

But Suneda was coming to see him today. Billie did not nor could not think of anything else but her. It was their day, the special time to see each other, if only for a short period.

It took Suneda about a month after they had met, but she did finally come to see him. They had started out by writing each other. Suneda had sent the first letter just a week after Billie had arrived at the prison. It was like a message from heaven for Billie. He had never gotten a letter from anyone before, let alone someone as lovely and interesting as Suneda. Then they wrote back and forth to each other each week, until he convinced her to come for a visit.

Somehow they had clicked that day at the courthouse and it had only gotten better since. He had even been making better progress with Doctor Scott. It took the doctor a while, but she finally figured out what had Billie smiling these days. She cautioned him to not get too serious too fast, but it was too late for that; Billie was in love and he knew it.

Suneda had been able to make it up to the prison a couple times a month for four months now, only two of which had included these conjugal visits. Billie had thought they were close before, but since they had started sleeping together, it was wonderful. Yes, the sex was great; Suneda had really opened his eyes to the the amazing world of a woman's body, but it was the other part of the act that really blew him away; it was a closeness, the intimacy he never imagined he could have with anyone. It was marred only by the fact that it was always under the eye of the perverted prick, Pete.

I can't wait to see her, Billie thought pleasantly as Pete escorted him to the spousal visitation block.

Except for Pete's annoying whistling, they continued down the long hallway to the visitation ward in silence. Nothing Pete could do today, even tempting him by teasing him into an outburst, would distract him from seeing Suneda. Pete would love for Billie to start a fight with him so he could deny Billie his time with her. It was just the way he was.

Suneda was in love with Billie too. The connection made at their arraignments was undeniable to Suneda. Eager to see each other, anticipating the touching and hugging, longing to kiss each other again, they had both lost sleep the night before, but it didn't matter. Their love was stronger, more powerful than any devilish, controlling pills haunting her past or any barbed-wire walls blocking his vision. They needed each other. Fate had meant them to be together, crawling over their struggles as one.

At the visitation center ward in the Huntsville State penitentiary, makeshift bedrooms were set up for married prisoners. Those on good behavior were awarded much-needed conjugal time with their spouse. It was a prison incentive policy enforced by Pete and concocted by Warden Stackhouse to keep convicts under control. It worked like a magic charm. Prisoners with a lover on the outside were complete pussies on the inside, whipped after a dip in the honey pot. They walked, mesmerized, back to their cells, smiling and purring all nice and calm from Stackhouse's playhouse.

Suneda had to sweet talk Pete, since Billie and Suneda weren't married, by giving him a few peaks so he would let them have their private time. It simply amazed Suneda what a $2.45-an-hour security guard wannabe-police officer would do, jeopardizing his job for a thigh-high panty look-see or a quick breast shot. Billie and Suneda suspected he saw even more but there was nothing they could do about it. Spending quality, intimate time together was worth letting Pete get his cheap, jolly shots off.

As Billie and Pete turned the last corner, Billie could see Suneda through the glass in the door that separated the prisoners from the visitors. She was sitting at the end of the hallway as always, waiting for him. She was looking down at her hands in her lap, a concerned look on her face. When they got close enough for her to see them, she looked up and plastered on a smile.

"Stay here, Billie. I'll open the door for her," Pete said.

Pete unlocked the door, stepped through, and let it lock behind him. He walked up to the room they would be staying in, opened the door on the visitor side, and waited for Suneda to step up.

Suneda knew what she had to do to keep the peace and ensure her time with Billie wasn't disrupted. As she passed by Pete, she gave him a flirtatious wink and he patted her firmly on her fanny. Suneda always made sure Billie didn't see the butt slap or anything else she let Pete do or see before she entered the makeshift bedroom, sure it would set Billie off.

Pete walked across the room and opened the prisoner door. He motioned Billie over.

Pete stepped up close to Billie before he let him in. "Five bucks, Billie, or you leave the door open for me," Pete instructed.

"What? Fuck you, Pete. Suneda gave you yours," Billie said angrily.

"The price went up. Inflation, buddy, it's everywhere. Everyone pays these days," Pete replied with a smile.

Billie reached into his pocket and felt the homemade steel shank he kept there. He fumbled with it briefly, toying with the idea of using it on the dumb fuck, then quickly located three crumpled up dollar bills he had left from his pay, working in the library. He gave the money to Pete.

"It's all I have. Now leave us alone or else," Billie snarled as he fondled the metal shank.

"Or else what, Billie? You gonna cry out loud for your mommy or should I say for your daddy, you big fucking baby? You don't demand anything here," Pete shot back, slapping his night stick in an open palm.

Billie squeezed the shank again as tight as he could, white knuckling it, preparing to draw it out if one more lame word came out of this dickhead. Thinking of Suneda inside waiting on him, he wisely let go of his grip. He took a deep breath, huffing and puffing while looking sternly back at Pete. He stepped into the room and slammed the door shut, rattling the small window in the room.

Suneda was lying on her back in the full-size bed with open arms, inviting him in as she lifted the sheet up to coax him next to her. Teasingly, she had taken her clothes off and was ready.

"Someday," Billie murmured out loud, "I'd like to slap Pete upside his head, kick his ass, shove that stick…" Billie said, grumbling as he crawled in the bed next to Suneda.

"What are you mumbling about, Billie, Who'll get his? What's the matter lover?" Suneda asked.

"It's nothing important. No worries, love. I just want to get out of this place."

"I know, that's what I was thinking too. It's only a little over four years, and maybe with good behavior…"

she trailed off as she started to unbutton his shirt. "That will have to wait for the time being. Now come closer and make love to me," Suneda said in a seductive, demanding voice.

"Yes dear," Billie said, smiling brightly as he took off his shirt. Suneda helped pull his pants off and urged him up on top of her.

Making love to Suneda was sweet, spicy, and hot. Better than being high. Not long after Billie arrived at the prison he had tried smoking some of the counterfeit pot that was smuggled into the prison, but since he had started seeing Suneda, he didn't feel a need for it. She gave herself to him, completely and without hesitation, fulfilling all his wants and desires. Anything he wanted, she would always say; she was a woman most men could only dream about.

"Billie, tell me what you like, anything you want, just tell me baby. Take me, I am yours," she would say in a sensual whisper in his ear "Tell me, my love." It took some coaxing, but Billie liked this approach very much. He had to give in.

"Do that again," he would demand, and Suneda happily accommodated the request with much energy and pleasure.

"Harder, harder, faster, faster now, feel me, Billie, give it to me, all of it. It feels so good, oh my…my goodness," Suneda squealed out in orgasm.

Peter the Peeper had his earplug suction-cupped to the door, listening in as Suneda gave way to her inner emotions. Pete got his rocks off that way, his sick, cheap fetish. As soon as they were finished, two knocks on the door was his signal that their time was almost up for the week.

"Ten minutes you two. Ten minutes; make it quick," Pete said through the door.

Suneda never asked questions about Billie's past. As he opened his heart and soul, she just listened and consoled him, promising to be with him forever, no matter where it may lead. She was an angel. She was Billie's angel.

Billie rolled on his side and stared at Suneda. "What's bothering you, Suneda?"

Suneda looked up with a start, obviously surprised by his question. "Nothing, sweetie. I'm fine."

Billie caressed her cheek. "You're not fine. There's something bothering you, I can tell."

Suneda looked down and bunched up the sheet in her fingers. "I'm so afraid Jorge is going to find me. The word on the street is he is going crazy loco trying to find me. He has his dogs looking everywhere."

The minute Billie heard Jorge's name, his heart started to race. Suneda had told Billie all about him. He was a Mexican drug lord named Jorge Espuma, better known as El Sanguinio, the blood luster. He had one of his underlings by the name of Pablo staged out at the Houston airport looking for young, good-looking foreign girls who came into the country seeking asylum or just a better life. These girls were coming to America to escape corruption, brutality, poverty, and frequently human rights violations of the corrupt governments they lived in. Women and children were most vulnerable. If they stayed in their home countries, they were likely to be raped or forced into slavery. America offered them hope for a better life, or so they thought. Once under Jorge's control, he would gain their trust by feeding them and giving them a place to stay, though he always kept them in isolation. He would also get them hooked on drugs, which gave him complete control over them.

When Suneda had run away from home, Jorge was looking for a virgin for his own to take. His last one had grown old and fat. He had many such women over the years. Each one he simply discarded whenever they no longer pleased him. When Pablo saw Suneda sneaking off the helicopter after the pilot and other passengers deplaned, he knew she was exactly what his boss was looking for.

Pablo had offered the scared newcomer a ride and a safe place to stay. Suneda was wary of the stranger, but he could speak her language and seemed friendly enough, so she reluctantly agreed. Once in Pablo's van, he drugged her and took her to El Sanquinio.

The drugs consumed Suneda. Her dreams of becoming a doctor became the horror story of a hallucinating drug addict. Jorge pumped her full of heroin, speed, acid, and amphetamines, keeping her under his power.

Suneda was forcefully coerced into becoming a listless sex slave and a drug mule for Jorge. She was his personal whore and an addicted mess. She moved his drugs to and from Columbia and Mexico for three years before being arrested. The police picked Suneda up while she was sitting on a park bench in the 5th ward on Houston's east side. That's when she met Billie. She had been hiding from El Sanguinio ever since.

Suneda began to cry. "I can't live in hiding anymore, always in fear of that filthy man drugging me and taking me as his sex slave again. Please, Billie, we have to do something soon, anything," Suneda whimpered.

Billie got a Kleenex off the nightstand and gave it to Suneda.

"El Sanguinio has an informant in this prison. I saw him in the visitation area when I got here today." Suneda started crying again. "He is going to tell Jorge I am here unless I pay him."

Billie sat up straight. "What's he look like?" Billie said through clinched teeth. He could feel himself losing control, but he had to keep it under wraps for Suneda's sake.

Suneda blew her nose. "He's short, about four inches shorter than you with a scar across his right cheek."

"That stinking little Mexican fucker. I knew something wasn't right with him. I have been seeing him around everywhere lately, like he is keeping track of me."

"He used to be in Jorge's inner circle before he stole something from him. He knows how much El Sanguinio is obsessed with me. He will tell him I'm here if I don't pay up."

Billie took a deep breath. "How much does he want?"

"He wants five hundred dollars."

Billie sat on the edge of the bed and ran his fingers through his hair. Suneda didn't have that kind of money and neither did he. She was working cleaning hotel rooms, putting what she could away for when he would get out. His job in the library only allowed him to save five maybe six dollars a week, after he paid for the things the prison didn't cover, like haircuts and the sweets he liked to buy for Suneda when she visited. But there was no way he was going to give that Mexican fuck five hundred dollars, even *if* they had it.

Billie turned back toward Suneda, who was now dressed and putting on her shoes. "Tell that Mexican you will bring him five hundred bucks when you come back next week to visit me," Billie said.

"I don't have five hundred dollars, Billie."

"Don't worry about that. Just tell him that. It will buy us enough time," Billie said.

There was a knock on the door.

"Five minutes you two lovebirds, five minutes…get it while it's hot…get it?" Pete said, smirking on the other side of the door.

"Suneda, listen closely," Billie whispered, ignoring Pete.

"We are going to leave here together very soon. Find us a place nearby where we can hide out for a few days. I'll figure out how to get out of here before you come back next week," Billie said.

There was another knock on the door.

"Time's up you two."

Billie stood and held Suneda by her arms. He kissed her hard, then pulled away with a small smile on his lips. "Don't worry, I'll figure it all out. I'll get out of here and then we'll be together for real, forever."

+

Jorge was pacing back and forth across the room, furious from the incompetence of his right-hand man.

"Where the hell is my sweet, Sunny bitch? It's been five months! You have brought me no clues? Nothing, why do I keep you around, Pablo? A simple task is all I ask, to find a low-life drug addict. Are you hiding her from me, Pablo?" Jorge screamed.

"No, no boss, she is yours, only yours. I don't know where she is, *Patron*." She was selling crack downtown. That was the last time I saw her," Pablo responded. "Maybe she got picked up and deported."

Pablo had found another virgin for Jorge after Suneda disappeared, but Jorge was obsessed with Suneda and made him continue to search for her. But she had disappeared.

"You were supposed to keep an eye on her, you stupid worthless ass. Why do I pay you?" Jorge said, pushing Pablo against the wall. "Find her before I do it myself, right after I cut your throat and dance in your blood," Jorge whispered in his ear.

Frantically, Pablo ran to the door to get out of Jorge's sight and El Sanguinio's reach.

Pablo doubled his efforts to find Sunny, the nickname Jorge had given Suneda. He had four soldiers scouring the downtown back-alley drug drop-spots, painstakingly looking for Sunny. They searched under overpasses, talked with the other whores, checked every empty overgrown lot for any clue of her whereabouts, thinking she might be living with the homeless, if she wasn't already sent back to whatever hellhole she had come from. Or perhaps she died weeks ago, shoveled into a dumpster and taken off to the landfill. Pablo didn't want anything to do with this last thought. If it were true, he knew he would be joining her soon.

Another four of Jorge's stooges were positioned at and around the Houston courthouse, police station, and the immigration building, looking and searching for answers because finding Suneda was Pablo's only chance to live. Jorge would have no mercy on him. Finally, a clue to her whereabouts came in.

CHAPTER EIGHT

TOSS AND TURN

Billie could not sleep, restless on the lumpy old mattress with worn-out pillows, trying to find a solution to his problem. He pulled the wool blanket over his head, trying to cover up the mindless chatter in his head.

I need to get the hell out of here, Billie thought as he rolled over on his side.

I need to get Suneda out of here. Take her home where she belongs. I have to protect her. Kill that fucker Jorge, if I have to.

Billie pulled the blanket down and rolled on his back, eyes wide open. *How the fuck can a crazy, low-life piece of shit live free without a care in the world, while I am in this shithole for defending myself against a dirty, filthy old man who got his kicks out of abusing a little boy? I just don't get it*, Billie angrily mused.

Then he started thinking about Suneda. Reliving Suneda's story made Billie feel sick. He didn't want to think about it anymore, yet he couldn't stop. It was eating him from the inside out. Billie sat up in his bunk. Time was up.

I have to get out of here before El Sanguinio finds Suneda again.

"What's the matter, Billie? Are you having that damn nightmare about your father? You know I'd kill him for you all over again if I could," Billie's roommate, Andy, said, poking the underside of Billie's mattress.

"I know you would, Andy, but I'm not thinking about that crap tonight. I've been thinking about Suneda. I have to get out of here, man, before I go crazy and lose my sanity. I have to save her. I have to save myself from this shithole. All I want is to have a normal, decent life in a peaceful place where I can't be found, to finally live my life, get married, and have a bunch of kids. Is that too much to ask?" Billie replied.

"No, not too much to ask at all, Billie. We all want a normal life. You don't even deserve to be in here, man. What you did was self-defense. There's no justice. This place will drive anyone insane. I can't sleep either. All I can think about is getting out of here tomorrow. It's been fifteen years, buddy."

"I am happy for you, Andy. You did your time, man.

I am going to miss you brother. I wish it were me going free," Billie said.

"If you stop beating the hell out of people, get your head screwed back on straight, and keep it there, Billie, you'll be out in a couple of years," Andy said.

"You're still going to help me, right? What we talked about. When I'm ready, I'll let you know."

Andy was a Korean War veteran trained in explosives and detonation devices. Andy and Billie were tied by blood as brothers. Andy knew of Billie's past. Billie knew of Andy's past. They bound by word to keep their most trusted secrets becoming close friends during their time in prison together holed up in their ten by twelve foot cage. As brothers often do when brought up in the same bedroom, they joked around often. They shadowboxed each other, but mostly they watched each other's back. They covered for each other every single day. The Huntsville State pen is no place to have enemies. Andy had his share, as did Billie. Friends were few and far between. They stuck together in a bonded brotherhood. The two of them were not to be messed with.

Andy was honorably discharged after he blew off all but two of the fingers on his left hand. A makeshift bomb detonated early when he was placing it up in a mine pod. Poof! Three fingers were gone just like that. The deafening sound left ringing in his left ear that nearly drove him crazy at times but he was lucky to be alive. The scars on the left side of his face gave him stature in the cell block. He looked like someone you didn't mess with.

Who really knew where those deep, grownover soft tissue cuts came from.

Like most veterans he came home to no fanfare, no parade or band, and no job. He did handyman work for a while. Over time, there was little work to be had for a one-handed handyman. Rather than starve to death on the streets, he decided to rob a bank. Twenty years to life is how his story goes. Andy was getting out early because of good behavior. He never once stuck a finger in an authority figure's eye, or anyone else's, for that matter. He was smarter than that.

"Right, man, whatever you need. Uncle Andy will be there for you. Just say the word."

CHAPTER NINE

ADIOS AMIGOS

Huntsville State Prison
Huntsville, Texas

Billie arrived in the prison's cafeteria, following in line with the rest of the pack of convicts in front of him. The despondent server scooped out a spoonful of dried-out scrambled eggs, some overcooked potatoes, two pieces of greasy bacon and stale, dry whole wheat toast. Billie picked up a cup of watered-down orange juice from the counter and headed for a table.

Knowing that the chow was not to his liking, he had to eat it anyway. He was hungry after his workout regime. Billie sat far away from the others and watched Pete chug down a glass of piss-warm milk and smiled.

The room was filled with buzzed-head, blue-shirted felons, chatting, and laughing as though they were staying at some damn country club.

Bunch of losers stuck here with no place to go. Rats in a dead-end maze. I guess they need to make the best of it. What else can they do?

He looked down at the disgusting mess on his tray. *Something is better than nothing.* He adjusted his mindset before he began to choke down his food.

I am definitely *not going to miss any of this shit!* He grinned while taking a stab at the potatoes with a plastic fork. He shoveled in the rest of the food while contemplating his escape again over and over in his head.

Today was it, the day they had been waiting for. Timing had to be perfect to pull it off. They both knew this. He visualized his moves, repeating every step one more time before getting up to go to his appointment with Dr. Scott. The background clatter of mumbled voices, shuffling feet, and banging dishes didn't distract him from his mission. He was tuned in to his future, tuned out of his past. The love of his life was counting on him. His soul mate would be on the outside waiting for him. Billie was not going to let her down. No how, no way.

He wiped off the remaining crusted-egg matter from his lips with a napkin, walked over to the dish wash line, and dropped off his tray. Billie looked around, analyzing the potential hazards. Everything appeared normal, even the scene across the room, where a couple of prisoners were getting into a scuffle. That summoned Pete and a couple other guards, who ran over to break it up. This was a common occurrence in prison life, nothing odd about it. Fights broke out over some of the simplest issues. Most of the time it was a power play to mark territory, like a dog does when it pisses on bushes and trees to let the other dogs know who's in charge and who's been around lately.

The fight ended and Billie headed over toward Pete.

"Appointment time, dickhead," Billie said.

Pete sneered at Billie but didn't say a word.

Billie turned around and headed down the hallway to Doctor Jean Scott's office escorted by Pete. They did not say a word to each other. The distain they had for one another was palpable throughout the suffocating, long walk down the narrow hallway. Billie's therapy session started promptly at 9:00 a.m. He had one hour to set things up, prepare himself, and execute his plan. Billie pushed the door open to the Doctor's office and walked in. He waited a minute then looked back out the door and down both ends of the hallway, first to see where Pete was going, and then to confirm no one else was nearby. Pete walked down the hallway a few meters to stand guard until Billie was finished with what Pete called his "head case call."

"Have a seat, Billie," she said quietly. Doctor Scott sighed and looked at Billie with frustration. She knew Billie.

"How was your night?" Doctor Scott asked.

Billie meandered over to a fake leather sofa directly across from the doctor and plopped down.

"Same old, same old crap, but no fights or nightmares last night, doc."

"That's a good thing, Billie. The fighting has to stop if you want me to recommend early release or special privileges to make your life in here more bearable," she said, trying to plead to his sensibility.

"You don't understand what it's like in here, doc. You have to fight to keep your life and your manhood. It's kill or be killed some days. Special privileges don't mean squat if you're dead."

"How does that make you feel right now, Billie?" Doctor Scott probed once again, digging deeper into his inner most thoughts. Doctor Scott always braced herself during appointments with Billie. She had to allow the uncomfortable feelings related to her own childhood, remembering her own nightmare to help her with what Billie was going through.

"It makes me feel like shit, shameful. It was my fault. It's like being preyed upon all over again. What did I do to deserve this life, doc? Did I make this happen? I pose these questions to myself hundreds of times a day. Hell yes or hell no, never a definitive answer. I have to always be prepared to protect myself because inside these walls, behind your perfectly decorated, everything-in-its-place office, man-whores with big dicks are ready to jump me. They heard of my past. They don't come alone, doc. They come as a force, a pack of sleazy rats looking to pleasure themselves."

"Just like you had to with your step-father? Is that the way it feels?" Doctor Scott asked, reaching in farther with trepidation.

"Come on now, doc; you know how I feel? You ask me the same questions every day. He sexually abused me until I was fourteen years old. Then I killed the bastard. You told me it was justice. Your father did the same bullshit to you. You know how it feels, don't you, Doctor. Except you're not in a cage, having to bare your teeth to survive or did you forget all that?" Billie said, hate obvious in his voice. But that was all a show. Actually, he didn't like to bring in her past but today he had to get her mind on other things. It was working so far. Doctor Scott was fidgeting in her chair.

"Of course not, Billie, I will never forget what happened to me as a child, but this isn't about me," Doctor Scott replied, trying to control her anger.

"Are my answers never good enough for you? Right now I want to punch a hole through your office walls, beat up each one and tear them down so you can easily see, no, make that, really see without those rose-colored glasses you have on, what the hell is happening outside those walls. Not inside me, inside this fucking prison," Billie said. Then he stood and pulled up the shades on the windows that lined the outside wall of her office, where guards with semi-automatic rifles paced back and forth.

"See those guys up there, Doc, with the scope rifles and see the razor wire running across the top of that electric fence? That's where I live!" Billie shouted.

"Calm down, Billie, just calm down. Let's change the subject and the tone. Let's talk about your girlfriend. What is her name again? Where does she live?" Doctor Scott said wanting and needing to start down a different path with Billie.

"The hell with that bull, Doc. Start talking about my girlfriend, really? No one said a damn thing when I was a little boy. They ignored it. My family, including my mother, all of them abandoned me. I was a baby, a child, a teenager, and I finally had to take matters into my own hands to stop it. You see, now as a man in here, no one cares either. Do you get that, doc? And by the way, I am not about to bring up my girlfriend ever; it's best you forget about it."

Doctor Jean Scott, backed up against her own walls, figuratively, adjusted herself in the overstuffed, upholstered chair covered with a faded, paisley pattern and quickly wiped away a tiny teardrop as it rolled down her cheek. As she regained her composure, she stared directly at Billie. Thinking of what her father did to her made her noticeably upset. Thinking about what Billie was telling her finally sunk in, realizing the predicament

71

he was facing. She resituated in her chair and then looked away. Billie knew he would get this reaction. It was simply part of his plan to catch her off guard today. He knew her oh so well. After six years of intense counseling, she and Billie were from the same dreadful abuse club. You never want to talk about such things, but when you do, the pain and suffering resurfaces. Sometimes briefly; sometimes for days.

Doctor Scott snapped out of the nasty thoughts creeping in from her past and came back to the here and now. Keeping her professionalism wasn't always easy with Billie. Sometimes she wanted to scold him. Other times she wanted to hold him. When he brought up her past, it was hurtful and painful. Doctor Scott didn't understand why Billie was being so cold today.

"We've had this discussion many times, Billie. We agreed not to bring my past into *your* sessions," Doctor Scott said in reprimand.

"Sorry Doc."

"You should be, Billie. You are a young man now. Your attitude is not going to get you out of here any time soon. You need to learn how to deal it. Accept the past and focus on the future. You are too young to give up and spend the rest of your life in here. An entire lifetime awaits you," Doctor Scott implored.

Billie knew now was the time to make his move. He had Doctor Scott feeling off base, testy, and uncomfortable.

"What future? I have no future!" Billie shouted.

"What do you mean, Billie? Of course you do."

"My head is screwed up. I can't stop the pain. It's real, doc. I've been in this hellhole for six years. You know they'll never let me out."

"You'll be here ten more years if you don't work this out," Doctor Scott said with a scolding tone, trying to get his attention.

"I know. I know, Doc. It just hurts." Billie played on.

Billie admired Doctor Scott. With all their sessions, she was actually reaching him deep inside, breaking down his defenses. Of course, Suneda helped. But he couldn't share this breakthrough with her. Today she had to believe he was regressing.

Billie would use this ruse to his advantage, to aide in his escape. He was sitting quietly in his chair. Not saying a word. Billie started thinking about the fact that he didn't know his mother. How could his mother leave him with Jake the pedophile creep when he was four years old, never coming back to help him, find him and free him from the human monster?

"You have to talk about it, Billie. Tell me again from the beginning. It's the only way out. You know I will help you," she insisted. Doctor Scott knew she had to get Billie to tell his story again. The more he talked about his life, the easier it would be to accept what happened and move on.

"There are other ways out, Doctor Scott."

"What do you mean?"

"I have told you my sick dream over and over. Why do you need to hear that sick shit? You sick too, Doc?" Billie jabbed.

"It's not for me, Billie. It's not about me. It's for you to deal with it straight up."

"No more, Doc. I am done with all this shit."

"What do you mean? You have to keep talking about it. Please, Billie, open up to me. It will help. It helped me."

Billie shouted. "Here we go again. You just don't get it!" Billie stood up from his chair, stared directly into Doctor Scott's brown eyes, then abruptly turned his head away.

"What are you thinking about, Billie?" Doctor Scott asked trying to calm him, get Billie back on track.

"You really don't want to know, Doc…really you don't."

"Yes I do, I really do," Doctor Scott insisted.

Okay, here goes then…you asked for it. I hate my mother. I can't stand the thought of her!" Billie shouted out angrily, thinking about how a mother let this happen to a young child.

"Why didn't she protect me? Why did she leave her son with a sick fuck? What kind of mother would do that? Why didn't she kill him herself, Doc? She had every chance to. Two point blank shots to the forehead, that's all it would have taken. Bang, Bang. That's what I did,"

Billie said pointing his fingers in a makeshift gun as he got up and proceeded to walk toward her.

"Calm down, Billie. Put your hand down. Take a deep breath. Why are you getting up?" Doctor Scott asked sternly yet in a soft-spoken way. She hadn't seen Billie in this state of mind in a long time.

"Take your seat, Billie, or I'll need to call the guard. Sit down, please," Doctor Scott said in no uncertain terms.

"We could have been free to do what mothers and sons do, whatever the hell that is," Billie cried out in his rehearsed anger. He followed up with a look of great distain as he peered directly into Doctor Scott's eyes.

"Please sit. Stop approaching me, Billie. You are out of line," she pleaded as Billie towered over her.

"I'll never know now what it would be like to grow up with a mother, will I, Doc? It's too late for me. She ran out on me. That, I can never forget or forgive. Do you think she wonders about my ordeal with the monster?" Billie yelled.

Deep down, Billie did not hate his mother. He didn't even know her. Of course, he blamed his stepfather, but not his mother. Billie wiped away a couple of tears and then cupped his hands over his face. He did not want Doctor Scott to see his feeble attempt at pouting.

"Billie, I'm sure she thinks about you every day, but you can't blame your mother for the sins of your stepfather. Please sit down," Doctor Scott demanded, pointing at his chair this time. Billie stayed standing.

"That's it," Billie said, bobbing his head back and forth. "Don't blame your mother for what your stepfather did. Yeah, Yeah, Yeah, Blah, Blah, Blah. I've heard it all before."

"Stop it, Billie. Why are you acting this way? This is not like you. You have come too far to act like this. You're way too upset right now. What's going on?" Doctor Scott demanded.

Clearly concerned, Doctor Scott raised her voice toward the door to get Pete's attention "Guard, I need you in here right away."

"Wish him well, Doc. I slipped Pete four laxatives in his morning milk shake. My guess is he is making good time bonding with the shitter about now," Billie laughed.

"What are you talking about, Billie?" Doctor Scott was confused.

"I don't know who I am, Doctor, that's the point," Billie quipped. Then he reached down from above her and put his hands over her mouth to keep her quiet.

Doctor Scott struggled and kicked, surprised and startled by Billie's behavior. She tried to pull his hands off her face but it was useless; Billie's strength was overpowering. He pulled off the flowered scarf she was wearing, stuffed it in her mouth, and tied it around her head, wrapping it twice. He removed his shirt and ripped it down the middle and proceeded to tie her arms behind her back and her legs to her chair.

"I am sorry, Doctor Scott. I have to move on with my

life. This is the only way for me. I need you safe and out of harm's way," Billie said softly to her as he checked the ties to make sure they weren't too tight so as to not hurt his Doctor Scott.

As she looked into Billie's eyes, Doctor Scott could see he was determined to change his situation, taking matters in his own hands again as he did with his father six years ago. His quest for freedom and a more normal life drove his desire, nothing less simple or more complex, nothing more honest or pure. In her mind she wished him the best, as she always had.

"I love you as a son loves his mother, Doctor Scott. You should know I have found my true love and soul mate. I need to be with her. We are planning to be together for the rest of our lives," Billie said, his voice faltering. He was choking up, holding back tears, recognizing he may never see her again. Doctor Scott made him right. He was ready to go out and tackle the world.

Proudly sitting upright as tears began swelling in her eyes. Doctor Scott cried; tiny silvery pearls slid down the side of her cheeks as the realization set in. Billie was ready to face his future without her.

I love you too, Billie, more than you will ever know. Doctor Scott lowered her head in a prayer for Billie's safety.

Taking one last glance back at Doctor Scott, Billie smiled at her and left her office.

"No looking back this time, Doc. I don't want to live like this anymore," Billie yelled back so Doctor Scott could hear.

Doctor Scott struggled with her constraints and eventually freed herself.

"Billie, please stop!" She knew he was probably long gone but she had to try. *This isn't good for you.* "We can talk through this. This is not the way."

Dropping the restraints on the floor, she pushed the chair aside and rushed out the door behind him in a futile attempt to reason with him. Frantically, she looked around for Pete.

"Pete. Pete…where the hell are you? Security! Security!" Doctor Scott yelled out in panic mode.

She ran back inside her office, pulled the receiver up from its base and called 011, the number to call for emergencies and other incidents.

"This is Doctor Scott. We have a run off. It's Billie Jensen. Please don't hurt him."

Billie picked up his pace to gain as much distance as he could. He thought about Doctor Scott with fondness, but it was time for him to move on without her, and she helped him do that.

The only reason I'm in here is because of that sick creep. "I was his son." Billie clinched his fists. Thinking about his stepfather's torrid abuse made him feel sick to his stomach. He shook his head to rid him of the thoughts.

I'm wasting time thinking of this stupid shit. Remember what Doctor Scott said. The past is gone. Breathe. Refocus.

Thinking about Doctor Scott made him question his plan as he made the last left turn, heading for the west wing of the ward. At the end of the hall was a door that would lead him to freedom and the start of a new life, away from the demons of his past and toward the love of his life, who waited anxiously for him on the outside.

Just thinking of Suneda made him run faster. He had to run, to protect Suneda and their dream. For Billie it meant leaving the dungeon he crawled out of, the pit that had buried him in over his head the past sixteen years. For Suneda it meant a life free to live on her own terms. But there were risks, big risks, for both him and Suneda. If he didn't make it out now, Jorge was sure to catch up with Suneda. And if Jorge let her live, she would never see the light of day again. If he was caught, he'd be sent back, only to get out when he had turned old and gray. They'd both be imprisoned one way or the other. It wasn't an option.

As he was running the last leg of the hallway, to the bright light at the end of the tunnel, the security alarms started going off. The place was going into lockdown.

Billie sprinted toward the door and turned the handle just as the lock clicked into place. But he was through. He ducked next to the dumpster as two armed prison guards zipped past him. They were scanning every inch of the building perimeter as they ran by him with their guns drawn.

Billie's plan was simple, so simple it was scary. He watched each day as the trash containers were rolled out of the west wing door at exactly 10:00 a.m. and emptied into dumpsters. Billie couldn't believe his eyes when he first observed it; the trash truck would pull up to the last dumpster, pick it up, and empty it out. All he had to do was jump inside the dumpster before the truck arrived and he'd be out before anyone figured out where he had gone. It would be so easy. Billie often wondered what they would do to Warden Stackhouse, the fat fuck, considering his lack of oversight on such an obvious lapse in security. *Why hadn't any other inmate seen it before me?* Or had they been itching to make their move just like him, waiting, biding their time. Once Billie had decided he needed to leave, he was so afraid someone else would escape this way before him. Billie's life hadn't been lucky or blessed thus far, but that was about to change, he was sure of it.

After the guards ran by, Billie went for the lid. He stood and shoved on the metal top, but it didn't budge. He tried again, harder this time. Still no luck. He scanned the rim of the lid and found what was holding it in place, a latch, a latch closed by a keyed lock. He was screwed.

Billie hit the lock hard with his hand. The hard metal cut into his palm but he didn't even flinch.

Looking around, he saw the large, green Bayou City Sanitation truck with the open-mouthed alligator painted on its side, driving down the road outside of the chain link fences. He had to think of something quick.

Billie ran around to the back of the dumpster and straining with all his might, he pried it away from the wall enough for him to get in behind it.

Maybe I can overpower the guy, make him drive me out, he thought. It wasn't the best plan but he didn't know what else to do. There was no going back inside, that was for sure.

The dump truck was let in past both gates and had pulled up in front of the metal container Billie was hiding behind.

The reverse beeper started when the clutch was released as the driver grinded it into reverse. The truck stopped inches from the dumpster. The driver got out, unlocked the top, and flipped it up against the wall above Billie's head. Then Billie had a better idea. *This is my chance*, he thought, his heart racing.

And as the driver headed back to his cab, Billie swung himself up and over into the piles of garbage bags. The hydraulic arms were maneuvered in place and the container rose in the air and deposited Billie and the garbage into the cavernous compartment behind the truck's cab. The truck was almost full so Billie didn't sink down very far.

It's all downhill from here, Billie thought as he

relaxed into the plastic bags all around him, finally able to breathe. It was hot and stunk to high heaven: rotten, moldy food, refuse from hundreds of bathroom waste cans. He didn't want to think about what was all around him. But the worst part was over. He could see the smile on Suneda's face. He could almost feel her in his arms. Billie smiled and closed his eyes.

The truck started moving forward, toward freedom, toward Suneda. Then Billie heard a low creaking sound, like metal scraping against metal. He lifted his head and noticed the bags around him were moving, moving together, moving closer, nowhere for him to go. The driver was compacting the trash.

CHAPTER TEN

A GOOD SAMARITAN

Houston, Texas

Although Billie didn't know it, his mother never stopped looking for him. She never gave up hope, not even in a million years. She prayed she would find him someday alive and healthy, maybe raising his own family. She called the detective in charge of his missing person case every week for updates, even when she was in the institution. When she couldn't call, she had someone else call for her. Elana didn't want the police to give up on Billie, on her, or file Billie's case in the cold-case section of the police files.

"I am sorry, Elana. We don't have any new

information on Billie. I will call you if something turns up." The detective repeated this statement every time she called.

Elana held a vigil in Billie's memory every year on his birthday. Although little news came of Billie for over ten years, she held onto her faith that one day she would find him safe and happy.

Elana was jumpy every time the phone rang, fearing it was terrible news or hoping she would hear that he was found unharmed and safe. The anxiety was excruciatingly painful at times. Elana jumped up from the kitchen chair as the first ring bellowed out from the phone.

"Ms. Jensen, this is Detective Miller calling."

"Yes, Detective. Have you found my Billie?"

"No ma'am. I am afraid I don't have good news for you," the detective said with as much empathy as he could.

"What do you mean? Oh my God, Detective, what is it? What happened to my son? Is my Billie dead?" Elana cried out in horror.

"We don't know that for sure, ma'am. We ran some more traces on Jake Jensen. We crosse-referenced some open case files with the FBI in Missouri, Kansas, and Arkansas. It appears he also goes by the name John Jensen, aka, Johnny Jacob Jensen." Detective Miller abruptly stopped talking as he searched his mind for the right words to use.

"Johnny Jensen? Tell me what you found out," Elana pleaded with him, demanding answers.

"I am sorry to have to tell you this, Ms. Jensen... but..."

"But, but what? Tell me what the hell is going on. You owe me that much, Detective."

"We suspect Jake Jensen has been involved in the abduction and killing of at least three young men. We've followed credible leads with the same MO. He lived in Missouri, Kansas, and Arkansas, in trailer parks at the time the three boys went missing. They were abducted when they were toddlers, only to be found dead at around fourteen years old." He hesitated again. "All of them were sexually abused for years before they were found."

"Oh my God! How can that be?" Elana broke down. She started to shake violently, uncontrollably, her hand hardly able to hold onto the receiver. She felt as if she was going to pass out. Taking a deep breath, she fought it off, determined to be strong no matter what.

Elana was now feeling sick to her stomach. Then a comforting thought occurred to her.

"Billie is only thirteen now, Detective. Does that mean my Billie is still alive?" Elana cried out with a glimmer of hope in her voice.

"We don't know, Ms. Jensen."

"You have to find him, Detective. For the love of God, you have to find him and bring him home safely to me. And please stop calling me Ms. Jensen," Elana said.

"Yes, ma'am, I am sorry about that. I'll keep you informed if we find out anything new."

"Thank you. I'd appreciate that."

Elana hung up the phone and broke down once more.

The Good Samaritan who saved Elana the night Jake left her for dead in the drainage ditch was a mother by the name of Mary Smithers. She was married to Jake before he married Elana. Jake had run off with her son Jimmy. She had been following him, tracking him, trying to find him to bring him to justice. Mary Smithers and Elana became good friends, a sort of support group of two.

Elana regretted not killing Jake when she had the chance, during one of his drunken stupors. But back then, she didn't know what kind of creep he really was. Guilt was overwhelming on most days, but she had no choice. She had to move on with her life, praying for Billie along the way. She cried herself to sleep on many nights when sleeplessness would finally give way to fatigue.

CHAPTER ELEVEN

TWO DICKS AND A DOCK

Huntsville State Prison
Huntsville, Texas

The prison was on high alert, alarms blaring, lights flashing, a real lockdown. Guards, authorities, everyone who was anyone was scurrying about, covering their own ass, pointing fingers, trying to figure out what the hell happened to Billie Jensen. How did he get out? Where was he? Where did he go?

"This is Warden Stackhouse from the B Unit in Huntsville, Holiday unit. I need Texas Ranger Detectives Logan and Morris to get to the prison now. We have a code green on our hands. Get over here as soon as you can, over," Warden Stackhouse communicated over the radio.

Code green was the prison's secret message dispatch for a jailbreak. Code names were used all the time in these matters to keep certain situations, like an escape, under wraps just in case some reporter was listening in on a police band radio. They had a runner, a mister Billie Jensen. This would not be good for Stackhouse. He needed to get this quickly under control. Stackhouse was already under scrutiny with the Board of Prisons for his lackadaisical management style, questionable ethics, and spousal conjugal policy. The longer they could keep this out of the public eye, the better for all concerned.

Detectives Danny Logan and Jackie Morris arrived at the warden's office at 11:00 a.m. Warden Stackhouse directed them to take a seat.

"So who skipped town?" Jackie asked, a slight grin on her face.

Stackhouse frowned. "A relatively new kid by the name of Billie Jensen," he said as he sat down in his office chair.

"How did he get out, Stack?" Danny asked.

"We saw him on surveillance video. He got into a trash dumpster around 9:30 this morning and the truck drove him right out the front gates. There's only a five-second window for him to pull it off. Can you believe it?" Stackhouse murmured quietly.

"You're fucking kidding me," Danny said as he shook his head.

"What was the kid in for?" Jackie chimed in.

"He murdered his old man when he was only fourteen,

blew him away point blank with a Glock. It was real nasty; that's what I heard. There was bloody and gooey shit all over the place," Warden Stackhouse explained. We got him from Juvy. He was working with a psychologist by the name of Scott and was supposedly making progress but he still had anger issues. That's what landed him here. Another inmate at Juvy said the wrong thing and the kid broke his nose and beat him up pretty bad.

"Why would a kid kill his old man?" Jackie asked.

"That don't matter right now, Morris. We, I mean you and Logan need to bring him back in fast. I don't give a rat's asshole if he is brought in dead or alive. Just get him back here ASAP," Warden Stackhouse said sternly.

"Any known accomplices?" Jackie asked.

"His shrink thinks probably his girlfriend, Suneda Ortega."

Stackhouse shoved a grainy picture of a pretty young girl with long dark hair at them along with Billie's mug shot.

"We got that picture of her off a prison camera. She came to visit him pretty often."

Danny picked up the picture and did his best wolf whistle. "I'd escape for her myself. Shit, Stack, how did you miss this one?

"Just get him back or we're all in the shithouse," Stackhouse shot back.

Detectives Danny Logan and Jackie Morris were ten-year veterans. They were Texas Ranger special agents assigned to the Bureau of Prisons for just such incidents. They were rookies when they first met at the Outpost, a bar frequented by the Rangers, FBI agents, and CIA operatives. Danny Logan was thirty and built like a body builder. His crew cut amplified his tough guy image. Ms. Jackie Morris, a slender redhead, only a year older, had always been attracted to the strong silent type. Even though he was four inches shorter, Logan fit the bill nicely. After several Black Russians, Jackie took Danny back to her place. They had a lot of sex in a lot of places in her apartment all night long. A headache and a hangover later, Jackie regretted her choice, especially the day they were assigned as partners two years later.

Shit was going to hit the fan soon if they didn't find the Jensen kid and they both knew it. Their jobs were on the line. There was no political appetite for having escaped convicts running around the city causing fear throughout the population.

"Listen to me, Logan," Warden Stackhouse said. "There's no time to jam me up; we need to find him and bring him back before all hell breaks loose. We are all on the line for this. Don't forget the chain of command; you know which way the shit will roll. If they jump down my ass, yours is going to be up for grabs too, quid pro quo. You understand me Logan? Are you listening to me Morris?" Warden Stackhouse barked.

"Yes. I don't like it but I get it," Jackie said as she nodded her head.

"Good."

"So even though your ass is big enough for both of us, Morris and I will institute protocol right away." Detective Logan stood, saluted with a Nazi two-finger salute, and clapped his heels together.

"Yeah, yeah, yeah, you're a real funny man. Now get the hell out of here and go do your fucking job," Stackhouse said.

Morris knew they were in deep trouble if they didn't bring Jensen back in before nightfall. They called out the dog patrol, two helicopter units, and a dozen squad cars to aide in the pursuit. Dog patrols worked out from the fence line in six directions, working 360 degrees, extending out in a back and forth sweeping pattern. They would cover a ten- to twelve-mile swath from the prison grounds. It was the best way to cover a lot of ground in a short period of time. County Sheriff deputies were dispatched from Chambers, Montgomery, Harris, Fort Bend, Liberty, and Walker counties to set up road blocks on the major roads, interstates, and highways within fifty miles of the prison. The police departments of Huntsville, Conroe, Dallas, Tyler, San Antonio, Austin, Corpus Christi, and Beaumont were made aware of the pending situation that could be headed in their direction.

Officers were instructed to stop and search all cars. They were on the lookout for a white male, six feet tall, two hundred and ten pounds with blue eyes and a prison crew haircut. His accomplice was female, dark complexion, black hair with brown eyes and approximately five feet tall, a tiny one who barely pushed one hundred pounds.

State Troopers were sent to Houston, Hobby, and Ellis field airports. All bus lines, cruise lines, Amtrak, Union Pacific railroad, and taxi companies were given descriptions of the perpetrators. Local television and radio stations were notified and given a press briefing by Stackhouse. The Port of Houston Authority and the Houston Ship Channel were put on high alert. An all-points bulletin was in effect, with a shoot to kill order if necessary. This was a city, county, and statewide lockdown. The detectives' first stop was Bayou City Sanitation, they had a driver to interview. They were all tracking a convicted killer. Everyone was put on high alert.

CHAPTER TWELVE

CHEESEY WEASELS

Sam Houston National Park Campgrounds
Conroe, Texas

J ust as planned, Suneda pulled the stolen blue Chevy sedan up next to the side of the garbage truck after it pulled into the Shipley's donut store. It was always the third stop after the prison. Suneda watched as the chubby driver exited the dump truck and hobbled into the store to get some donuts and coffee. The garbage man looked back toward the prison when he heard sirens blaring in the distance.

Suneda got out and tapped the side of the truck with her car keys, letting Billie know the coast was clear.

"Billie, let's go," Suneda whispered.

There was no reply.

Suneda looked at her watch. *It's the right time*, she thought. *Maybe he didn't get out, but all the sirens were going off. Something must have happened.*

She rapped again, harder this time.

She heard a loud thump and she jumped, surprised by the response but relieved nonetheless.

Billie's head popped out of the top of the truck.

Cautiously, looking around back and forth Billie crawled out over the top, down the side, and into Suneda's waiting embrace.

Keeping her eye on the donut-eating garbage man all the while, Suneda gave Billie a welcoming hug as he landed in her arms.

"You scared me. I thought something happened."

Billie closed his fist tight so Suneda wouldn't see his cut. "Something almost did…"

Suneda's eyes went wide.

"What?"

"Let's just say, me and an old office chair got real chummy; he saved my life." Billie said with a grin.

Suneda shook her head, not getting his inside joke, then decided he wasn't going to tell her any more so she leaned into him again. "You smell like garbage," Suneda replied.

"Thank you. I soaked in it just for you," Billie said, laughing while taking pieces of rotting vegetable, fruit peels, and other unknown objects off his shirt.

Billie touched Suneda's hair. "You cut it and changed the color," he said, surprised. Her silky, long black hair was now cut just below her ears and a mousey brown.

"I thought it would be a good idea. Do you like it?"

"I wouldn't care if it was a buzz cut and dyed purple," he said pulling her in close again, but we have to go. Now," Billie said as he took the keys. He opened Suneda's door and walked around to the driver's side to get in.

"You're such a stinking gentleman," Suneda said playfully as they drove off heading north on Interstate 45. They ditched the blue Chevy in a parking lot across from City Hall in downtown Conroe where Suneda had a Ford van parked, waiting there to make the switch.

A significant part of Billie's plan was to hide nearby in plain sight and not draw attention to themselves. Sam Houston National Forest was fifteen miles from the prison, just outside the dog sniffing circle.

Billie pulled into the campground at 10:35 a.m., unpacked the van, and pitched the tent Suneda had stowed away for them. They put it up in a somewhat secluded area at the end of a turnaround in the back of the campground. It was Friday and other campers were just starting to show up for their weekend visit. Suneda help Billie shave his head, then gave him a baggy tie-dyed shirt that hung past his hips and a goatee she bought at a costume shop. A fake ear stud in his right ear and he was all set.

At about noon, another couple pulled in with a Winnebago two sites down from them. The campers smiled and waved at Billie and Suneda as they got out of their vehicle. Billie and Suneda waved back.

"I guess everyone wants to be where nobody knows who or where you are. This gigantic campground and those two pull right up next to us. There must be a thousand open spaces here to pick from," Billie huffed.

"What should we do, Billie?" Suneda asked, pretending to pick up sticks for firewood.

"Just act normal. We're here for the weekend, just like they are. Tell them we are from College Station," Billie said in a whisper.

"I don't know anything about College Station, Billie."

"No need to worry, princess. Just follow my lead."

"Oh my God, they're walking over here," Suneda said anxiously.

"Hello neighbors. I'm Joe Sullivan and this is my bunny girl, Beth," The man said as he reached out to shake Billie's hand.

"It's nice to meet you," Billie said, taking Joe's hand.

Joe had a good strong grip with skin coarse and rough, like sandpaper. *A working man's hands*. Billie wondered for a moment if Joe was a farmer or an oil rig man.

"I'm Tom and this is Sarah. We came down from College Station for a couple of days; had to get away from all the hustle and bustle of the big city, chill out some," Billie said.

"Yes, nice to meet you," Suneda added.

"It's like, for sure with me too," Beth said.

"What brings you two out here?" Billie asked.

"We come down to Texas in the fall to enjoy the color changes along the way. We're from Madison, Wisconsin. It's getting pretty chilly up there, had some snow flurries just before we left," Joe said.

"It's like, we love the State of Texas. We spend the whole winter down here visiting different campgrounds. Can ya dig it?" Beth said.

"One of our favorites is right there in College Station. It's off Highway 6. It's the one with the picture of a Possum on the sign. It's a KOA campground I think. I don't remember the name though. It's been a couple of years ago," Joe said as he took off his baseball cap and scratched his head.

"I think it's called Possum Hollow," Suneda said as she winked at Billie.

Billie didn't like all the small talk. Suneda was making stuff up, and it was going to get them into trouble

"It's something like that," Billie said.

"We'll let you get settled in and catch up with you later," Suneda told the Sullivan's as she turned to walk back toward their campsite.

"Sounds like a good plan. We'll kick up a fire later, chill out, and chug down a few cold beers. I've got some Molson's from Canada," Joe said. "Come by, if ya want."

"Thanks for the offer, but we've got other plans," Billie said and he put his arm around Suneda's shoulder.

"I get ya," Beth smiled. "Catch ya on the flip side,"

she said, then she and Joe turned around together hand in hand and began walking back to their campsite. When they were about twenty feet away, Joe turned back and asked them a question.

"Did you get the skinny about that escapee from Huntsville State Prison? It's all over the police band radio like, wow man."

"No, we haven't heard a word about it. We've been camping a week and we, like, unplug when we're out here," Billie said.

"Far out, man. I gotcha!" Joe said, giving them the okay sign with his hand. I'll see what I can find out over the radio. We'll let you know if anything is going down."

Everyone could hear the dog hunt off in the distance, barking in packs and then finally fading back as the sun went down. Two helicopters flew over them a half dozen times, shining sweeping spotlights down on everyone in the fading light of the day. Then there was nothing. Everything was quiet as the day turned pitch black. The campers hurried to get their campfires going.

Billie kept thinking about his escape plan. He knew that most escapees didn't make it past seventy-two hours because they didn't have a solid plan or any help on the outside. Not for Billie and Suneda. This was their chance for a new life together. While Billie was crafting his escape from the inside, Suneda had the outside escape details covered. The blue 1967 Chevy sedan was a decoy. She paid cash to an undocumented immigrant and switched license plates with an unsuspecting suburban housewife two days earlier. With the help of a friend, Suneda stole a brand spanking new white 1975 Ford van off a Ford car dealership lot, chancing it wouldn't be noticed as missing for at least a couple days. Switching dealer plates randomly on ten identical model white vans parked on the lot, she figured to confuse the car prep guys and buy them another day or two. In a few days the manhunt would become less intense. Billie and Suneda had their campsite set for the night, ready to finalize their plan.

The two would-be campers were ravished to the point of feeling starved. They had not eaten anything since the early morning hours. Since this was Billie's first time tackling a grill, Suneda was happy to help. Billie smiled at her as he yielded the fork and tongs to her outstretched hand.

"You are my queen," Billie said, pulling her close.

"How would you like your steak cooked, King Billie?" Suneda asked, smiling back.

"Rare. I like it rare."

"That's what I thought, but we have to let the charcoals turn white first," Suneda explained.

"Whatever the cook says works for me."

"I have an idea, Billie," Suneda said from out of nowhere.

"What's that?"

"I just happened to meet up with my Uncle Negos a few weeks ago. He runs a shipping business between the

Port of Limon in Costa Rica and Beaumont. I told him our story and he wants to help."

"Help us how?"

"He said we could stow away on his boat, hide in a shipping container on his next run into Beaumont. He'll get it set up for us."

"Your Uncle Negos will do that for us? Why would he do that? He doesn't know me," Billie questioned.

"Oh, Billie, I told him everything about you. How I want to go back to Alta Vista. How I want you there with me. I told Negos we were in love. We can raise our family there. Negos said he would take us. He wants to go home, too. He's ready to go back. He knows about Jorge and all the sick things he did to me. You just have to ask him man to man. That is the way it is in my culture. Please, please take me home to Alta Vista. You'll love it there." Suneda implored.

"What's it like there? Billie asked.

"It's beautiful, Billie. With all the flowers, the trees, the birds, the mountains, and the waterfalls, we can be one with nature in Sibo's world."

"Who is Sibo?"

"He's our God, who we pray to.

"You will love my family, too. We are a close-knit group, very close you'll see. We'll never look back, I promise," Suneda said.

Suneda looked so confident as she talked of her home and her people, Billie couldn't help but agree with her plan. "How far do we have to go?" Billie questioned.

"It's about fifteen hundred miles. Negos figured it will take three weeks to get us there. First by Negos' boat, then hiking through the rain forest and navigating the rivers," Suneda explained as if it were just a jaunt through the park.

"Is that what you truly want, seriously? What about being a doctor?"

"Yes, yes, yes, Billie that is what I truly want. Now that I've met you, nothing else matters," Suneda said, her voice breaking.

Billie looked at Suneda and sighed. He didn't want her to give up on her dream of being a doctor, not even for him. But first, they had to get free; he'd figure out the rest later. "And Negos will help, you're sure of it?" Billie asked.

"Yes, I know he will. He told me so. Negos wants to get me as far away from El Sanguinio as possible. Jorge will never find us there. Negos knows I am still in danger if I stay here. He loves me. Uncle Negos will be back in two days. If we are there, he will take us home." Suneda wiped a tear off her cheek.

As she began to cry, Billie held her close and told her everything would be all right.

"We'll head to Beaumont the day after tomorrow and I'll ask Negos, man to man, to take us to Alta Vista," Billie said.

"Thank you! Thank you, my sweet Billie." Suneda snuggled into his arms as they watched the coals slowly turn from black to a dusty gray.

"Do you think we will actually make it?" Suneda said in a quiet voice.

"Yes, we'll make it. It won't be easy, but as long as we stick together we'll make it. We only have to escape the authorities, cross the Gulf of Mexico, hike for miles and miles through treacherous terrain, raft down raging rivers, and elude wild man-eating animals and poisonous biting reptiles without getting caught or killed. Other than that, it should be a piece of cake," Billie said sarcastically.

"Oh Billie, it will be all right. We'll be in Sibo's hands."

"I am sure we will make it then, Suneda. This is our path. We have no other choice. There is no second guessing, no turning back," Billie told her with confident authority. Billie had a strength about him and an air of invincibility that Suneda admired. Feeling safe at last, Suneda pulled him close.

"Billie, take me now, make love to me," Suneda whispered in his ear.

"Aren't you hungry?"

"Just for you." Suneda stood and pulled Billie up next to her. He picked her up in his arms and took her to their tent.

Staying put for the next two days, mingling with Joe and Beth Sullivan and some other campers who were staying in the national forest was part of their cover to blend in and not draw attention to themselves. Everything seemed normal. Joe and Beth came by each night. They shared stories while roasting marshmallows over an open fire. They ate, drank, and laughed together.

Their last day, Joe and Beth came by their campsite for one last visit. "Hey are you two lovers in there? Are you decent?" Joe whispered into the side of the tent, waking the two of them up. Suneda and Billie untangled themselves and quickly threw on their sweats.

"Yeah, we're cool. What's up, Joe? Give us a second here. We'll be right out," Billie said yawning. Suneda hurriedly brushed her hair back, checked herself in a compact mirror, and crawled out. Billie was right behind her. Joe was standing there. Beth was up next to him holding his hand.

"What's going on?" Billie asked.

"I heard over my CB radio, the fuzz is closing in on the jail breaker. How cool is that?" Joe announced.

"Did they say where they were or where they saw them?" Billie asked.

"So you heard there were two of them?" Joe said without giving a second thought.

"Something about a man and a woman accomplice. The other campers are worried too," Billie said as he tried to cover up his slipup.

"Like, maybe it's you and Sarah," Beth joked.

"Or you and Joe," Suneda said with a strained chuckle.

"Not us. We are too damn old to be jail breaking;

having a hard enough time just getting in and out of that fold-down camper. We are just boring semi-retirees who like to do a doobie now and then," Joe laughed.

"Backatcha. Sounds like us too," Billie said, playing along.

"Hey, we're not old," Suneda said, giving Billie a playful slap.

That evening Billie and Suneda continued the pretention of enjoying their neighbor's company, drinking beer and Strawberry Fields Boones Farm wine until around midnight. During their goodbyes, phone numbers were exchanged with the Sullivans.

"Good night, Tom and Sarah, perhaps our paths will cross again someday," Joe said sincerely.

"Like, it's such a bummer you two are leavin' us tomorrow," Beth said groggily as she stretched her legs out one at a time. Joe helped Beth to standing, and they stood by the campfire and kissed as if Suneda and Billie weren't even there.

"Peace, man," Joe said, giving them the peace sign. Joe took Beth's hand and they walked clumsily back toward their campsite.

Billie zipped up the tent screen and closed the flap and then lay himself out next to Suneda. They lay in silence, listening to the sounds of the night. Billie still couldn't believe he was on the outside. He hadn't heard night sounds in a very long time: the rustle of the wind through the trees, the croaking of frogs, the haunting hum of the cicadas. He could see the thousands of pricks of light in the night sky even without looking outside his tent. It was something he had memorized in his mind since they had come to the campsite. Memorized just in case. But he didn't want to think about that. He pulled Suneda close.

"Billie, do you think we will ever find happiness and live a normal life like Joe and Beth?" Suneda asked as she snuggled up next to his chest.

"I would not say Joe and Beth are normal people," he said and laughed. "But I know what you mean, and I certainly hope so. A life that we can live in peace and harmony, free from the past," Billie told her while caressing her arm.

"Kiss me good night, Billie."

At daybreak, before the Sullivan's awoke, Billie loaded up the van for the ninety-minute drive to the Port of Beaumont. With a bit of luck, sticking to the plan, Negos would be on the pier waiting for them. A strange self-reflecting silence carried them through the oak-lined park esplanade as Billie drove cautiously out of the national forest and turned left on Interstate 45, heading north. Eighty-six miles to go, Billie said to himself. Neither Billie nor Suneda spoke a word as they drove, afraid to speak out loud as if talking would somehow alert the authorities to their whereabouts.

"We only have seventy-one miles to go now," Billie whispered.

"We are on our way to freedom," Suneda said as they turned onto Highway 105 East, heading toward Beaumont. There were no signs of predators, no sirens, no cops. The road ahead seemed clear. Billie nodded in agreement. The plan was working thus far.

CHAPTER THIRTEEN

THE THIRD DEGREE

Texas Rangers Station
Conroe, Texas

Detectives Logan and Morris were given the third degree by Captain Eddie Tanner from his office at the Texas Ranger headquarters. Warden Stackhouse stood in the corner watching, listening, ready to jump into the exchange. Captain Tanner issued them an ultimatum. Either return with Billie Jensen before all hell breaks out or face a desk job for the rest of their careers. Stackhouse was in the shithouse, no matter what, and he knew it.

A few seconds later, the governor marched into Tanner's office with his security team in tow.

"How could this have happened, Stackhouse? Escaping in the fuckin' trash!" Governor Todd Branson yelled. "My re-election is on the line because of your blind, ignorant stupidity. How am I going to explain your incompetence? If this piece of shit Jensen isn't found, you're going down with me, Stackhouse. You'll be lucky to get a security guard job at a strip club when this is over, you dumb ass," Governor Branson blurted out.

"I understand, Governor," Stackhouse said through gritted teeth.

With a coy smirk on his face, Stackhouse murmured under his breath, "Dumb ass is as dumb asses are…"

"What was that, Stackhouse?" the governor demanded.

Detectives Morris and Logan stood silent, amused by the exchange.

"Nothing sir…Just thinking out loud, sir, gathering my thoughts. Logan and Morris are on it," Warden Stackhouse replied.

"And you think that makes me feel all warm and fuzzy? Jesus Christ, Stackhouse, just get it done," the governor said as he pushed the door open and stomped out of Captain Tanner's office.

"You heard the gov; go get it done, detectives, dead or alive," Warden Stackhouse said.

Logan and Morris set up a meeting with Doctor Scott at the prison to ferret out as many details as possible about Billie's life, his quirks, his girlfriend, anything that would give them a lead. They knew they only had a few hours to get a solid bead on Billie, any more time than that and they may lose him forever. Searching for clues to where Billie was heading topped the agenda.

When they arrived at Doctor Scott's office, the detectives noticed she was noticeably upset.

"Have a seat there, detectives," Doctor Scott said, pointing them to sit across from her on the sofa.

"Thank you, Doctor Scott. We heard you and Billie Jensen had a close relationship, is that correct, doctor? Jackie asked.

"Yes, that is correct, Detective. Billie was my patient. I had been working with him since he was fourteen years old, for over six years." Doctor Scott sighed.

"Did he give you any indication he was planning to escape?" Danny asked.

"No, not a word, even though he was acting strangely that day, he completely caught me off guard. I am devastated that he left, running off like that. There is so much more to do." Doctor Scott sniffled.

"Tell me about his girlfriend, Doctor Scott. Did Billie ever talk about his girlfriend?" Jackie looked at her notepad. "A Suneda Ortega."

"Who told you he had a girlfriend, Detective?"

"Warden Stackhouse. We also stopped by Billie's cell block on the way over here. Talked to his station guard, Pete. He let us into Billie's cell to take a look around. Pete said she was a real good looker," Jackie explained.

"Yes, I know Pete. All I heard is that she is a beautiful

young woman with black hair and a dark complexion with Hispanic or Latin features. I think she was from Central America. Billie never wanted to talk about her. Actually he insisted on it."

"Think, Doctor Scott. We need answers soon or we'll never find him," Detective Logan pressed.

"Why don't you just let him go? His life has already been ruined," Doctor Scott retorted.

"What do you mean, Doctor?" Detective Morris asked.

"You don't know?" Doctor Scott queried.

"All we know is that he killed his stepfather. It got pretty ugly. Lots of blood and brain matter scattered all over the crime scene. Then he got sent here because he did some damage to a fellow inmate at the juvenile detention center he was at," Danny said.

"The real crime was that Billie's stepfather was a serial pedophile who abused his stepson for years before Billie finally got the strength, the resolve, the courage he needed to kill his attacker!" Doctor Scott shouted out at them in disbelief. "How can you not know who you are hunting down?"

Morris and Logan looked at each other with raised eyebrows.

"Shit," Danny said under his breath.

"That's why we're here talking to you," Jackie said.

It took a few more hours of good investigative work

and Logan and Morris finally uncovered that Suneda was from Costa Rica. They looked up her criminal background history, her arrest for drug possession with orders for deportation back to her native country. Since Suneda was the only one that had visited Billie since his transfer to Huntsville, it seemed logical that she was the one helping him. The deportation order as written sent her back to San Jose, the capital city, for processing, eventually to find her way home to her village, somewhere in the interior. A place called Alta Vista.

"That's it, Logan," Jackie proclaimed.

"What are you talking about?"

"It's obvious, don't you see? They're heading to Costa Rica, to hide out, maybe find a new life, back to her hometown village. What better way to stay hidden, out of sight in some remote place out in the middle of frickin' nowhere."

"You got it; that's it. We need to contact the airports, port authorities, and border patrol down in Brownsville and Laredo. We have to seal this off now."

Jackie grabbed Danny's arm. "Are you sure you want to do this, Logan?" "What do you mean?" Danny asked.

"I mean seriously, Logan, considering all the shit, what he has been through, can you imagine? And Suneda… she probably came here looking for a better life and ended up working as some drug lord's sex slave, for God's sake. Maybe we should look the other way…let them go."

"We have to get Billie, Morris. What the hell, I

ain't pushing no damn pencils to erase someone else's problems, no matter how fucked they've been." Danny Logan looked at his partner and shook his head.

Jackie stood. "Let's go. We're running out of time."

She felt sorry for Billie and Suneda, but Logan was right, she had to push these thoughts out of her mind and do her job to the best of her ability.

✦

Elana Jensen was sitting on the sofa knitting a pair of socks when the phone rang.

"Hello, may I help you?" Elana asked.

"This is Detective Jackie Morris. May I speak with Elana Jensen?" Jackie was sitting in the airport, waiting to board her flight to San Jose with Detective Logan.

"This is she. What is this about?" Elana's mind was flashing mostly bad thoughts. The last time a detective called her out of the blue was to tell her they had given up the search for Billie, informing her they were keeping the case open but had to pull back their resources.

"Go on, Detective, I am listening," Elana said intently.

"I have some good news and then some not so good news."

"What are you saying? What happened? Is there something wrong?" Elana said. Her throat was going dry and she found it was hard to breath.

Detective Morris figured it was better to cut to the

chase, not string her along. That's what she'd want if her child had been missing for seventeen years. "We found Billie."

"You did what? You found my Billie. Oh my God. You found him, my, my little Billie? Oh my God. Where is he? I want to see him. Is he all right, Detective? Please tell me he's all right," Elana demanded.

"Slow down, Ms. Jensen. Let me speak," Detective Morris said.

"Yes, Detective, please go on, tell me everything you know." Elana's voice went silent. She felt like she was buried in a coffin underground as the walls were closing in around her. With her eyes shut, biting her lip, Elana held out hope for the best.

"Billie is alive. This is the good news. The not so good news is that he escaped from Huntsville State Prison and is on the run from the authorities. We believe he is trying to get to Central America, Costa Rica to be specific. Do you know anything about this?"

It took a minute for Elana to speak. She couldn't see anything in front of her as her eyes filled with tears.

"Are you there, Mrs. Jensen?"

Elana blew her nose and tried to calm her breathing. "Thank God my Billie is alive. Thank you, God, for finding my sweet little Billie," Elana rejoiced.

"Mrs. Jensen, do you know anything about this? Have you spoken to Billie?" Detective Morris asked again with a tougher tone in her voice that demanded an answer.

"Please don't call me Mrs. Jensen, Elana is fine. And

no, I know nothing of this. I have not seen or heard from Billie in seventeen years."

"Do you know his girlfriend, Suneda Ortega?" Detective Morris asked.

Elana blinked the water from her eyes. Suneda? "No, like I said, it's been a long long time since I've seen or talked to Billie, Detective. He was just a baby when his stepfather took off with him."

"Do you know why he was in prison or why he is on the run in Central America?" Detective Morris continued her line of questioning.

"Oh my, no, I don't. What did he do? Why was he in prison, Detective?" Elana asked.

"He killed his father, Jake Jensen," Detective Morris stated as a matter of fact.

"You mean he shot that son of a bitch stepfather?" She wanted Detective Morris to be clear on this fact.

"Yes. He killed his stepfather, I guess you're right," Detective Morris clarified.

Elana did not know what to say next. Her mind was searching for the next best answer. Every family had secrets. She didn't know how much Detective Morris knew.

"His stepfather was a monster, Detective. I would have killed him myself if I'd have known what kind of a… thing he was," Elana said, obvious contempt in her voice.

"I know the circumstances surrounding Mr. Jensen's death, Ms. Jensen. I feel badly for the tragedy that befell your family, but I have a job to do.

"You have no idea, Detective. You really don't have

a clue." Crying loudly, Elana tried to hide her sobbing behind the phone handle.

"Let me help you, Elana. Let me help Billie. Billie was under the care of a Doctor Jean Scott. She is a psychiatrist based at Huntsville Prison. Since Billie was a minor when he killed his stepfather, he was initially incarcerated at The Youth Village. Doctor Scott started working with him there. And when he transferred to Huntsville, so did she. I will send you her information so you can talk to her about what has happened to him over the past seven years or so," Jackie said.

"Thank you, Detective. Thank you."

"But if Billie tries to contact you, you need to call me right away. If my partner and I can get to him before the authorities do, maybe we can do something for him."

Elana listened intently, understanding what serious trouble her son was in.

"I will, I promise."

The women exchanged contact information and Jackie told Elana she would keep her posted on their progress when she could.

Excitedly, Elana paced around her small apartment in wandering wonder.

"My Billie is alive. Thank you God, my Billie is alive!" Elana said out loud, her voice echoing off the four walls. She could barely contain herself. She looked at Doctor Scott's number on the slip of paper in her trembling hand and walked over to the phone.

✦

Joe Sullivan abruptly sat up as if he saw a ghost. He was still zipped tightly up in his sleeping bag. He shot up so fast he woke Beth.

"What's the matter, Joe, you havin' some sort of a heart attack or somethin'?"

"No, nothing like that. I feel fine, Beth dear. I was thinking about something Tom and Sarah said. Something doesn't sit right with me about those two. What Tom said earlier when I asked him about the jail breaker has been irking me."

"Like, what'd he say?"

"He said there were two of them. That he had heard there was a female accomplice helping the jail breaker escape. I never told him there was a woman helping him, did you Bethy?

"No, I don't think so."

"Remember when we joked it could be them. It felt awkward for a second. Do you remember that moment, Beth?

"Like yes, of course I remember feeling like it could very well be them. We were pretty drunk, ya know."

"We'll call the Texas Rangers on that hotline they gave over the radio. Let them sort it out."

✦

"Logan, grab your coat and badge. We just received a hot lead on Billie Jensen. We are heading to Beaumont," Detective Morris yelled over to Logan, who was just coming out of the men's room shaking some water off his still wet hands.

"I am right behind you, Morris. Lead the way, boss lady," Logan said while side stepping to catch up to her on their way out.

CHAPTER FOURTEEN

PABLO, POOR, POOR PABLO

"Negos, my beautiful, sweet Negos," Suneda blurted out while racing up to him as he stood on the dock, not far from his boat. Suneda jumped into his arms.

"Please don't jump on me, Suneda, I am getting too old for that," Negos said jokingly. He pulled the young girl in for another hug.

"I missed you so much, my dear Negos," Suneda said when they finally parted.

"And just as much as I have missed you, my sweet little princess." Negos wiped a tear from his eye with one hand while he wiped the tears streaming down Suneda's face with the other. Mutual smiles took control as drying tears faded to a glow of happiness and joy.

Suneda grabbed Billie's arm. "This is Billie Jensen. The one I told you about; my true love and soul mate," Suneda said proudly.

"It's nice to meet you, Billie Jensen. Yes, Suneda has told me about you," Negos said as he reached out to Billie with his hand. They shook hands, then Negos pulled Billie in to a husky, smothering bear hug.

"Your past is your past, Billie," Negos whispered in his ear. "Your future is your future. If Suneda loves you, then you are bound to me like family. I will forever protect you both," Negos said sincerely.

Billie almost lost it. He never felt this kind of "family" closeness. He never knew it existed. He suspected his mother had loved him when he was small, but he only remembered bits and pieces of that time. Most of his childhood memories revolved around his stepfather, and those were never pleasant.

"Thank you, Negos. I love your little princess; she is my angel. I will protect both of you with my life if I have too," Billie said as he tried to hold back the strongest emotion he ever experienced.

"How did you escape from prison, Billie?" Negos wanted to know.

"It's a long story, but Suneda and I planned it together," Billie said.

"Why did you escape?" Negos pressed.

"I love Suneda. We want to spend the rest of our lives together in peace and harmony, away from all the evil and despair we've faced in our lives thus far. We need your help. Will you take us home?" Billie asked Negos, man to man.

"Suneda told me about your childhood. I am sorry you had to go through that. And she told me about El Sanguinio and everything she's been through. Of course I will help you. I want to go home too. I need forgiveness from my family," Negos said.

"Thank you, Uncle Negos!" Suneda said, and then she planted a big kiss on his cheek.

"Listen. Do you hear that? Siren's coming; the police are closing in. They must have followed you. Hurry now, we need to push off as soon as possible," Negos insisted.

Negos felt an instant closeness to Billie, a natural bonding of two men a world apart yet they had a common bond in their love of Suneda. It was like they were supposed to meet. Billie felt the same sort of feeling. It felt right in an odd sort of way. They looked at each other in immediate agreement as guys often do. They both looked at Suneda.

Billie, Suneda, and Negos headed down to pier ten. They climbed a ladder at the aft end of Negos' boat where the cargo containers awaited them. The breeze was crisp and fresh, offering the trio endless possibilities to start a new life for all of them.

✦

Pablo was frantically searching into Suneda's past life, going through court dockets at the county clerk's office for arrest records from the day she disappeared. He checked the deportation orders, fearing the little bitch may have been deported back to where she came from, meaning he would have to go get her.

"Jorge is not going to like this at all. She was ordered to go back to San Jose. Shit, I am fucked, really fucked," Pablo said out loud. The order rattled in his clenched fist. "If the bitch gets caught again, then they'll send her back for sure."

Pablo was driving the van back to report to Jorge when Pablo heard about the jailbreak at Huntsville. They described the male prisoner that escaped, then his gorgeously stunning accomplice. His inside man had told him that he thought Suneda was visiting a kid by the name of Billie Jensen but he hadn't been able to confirm it yet. Pablo saw this as his last hope for bringing her pretty ass back or face the gauntlet of Jorge's wrath.

Pablo's suspicions were correct. Sunny and Billie's pictures were all over the news channels. Their escape hit the front page of the newspaper. At least he knew they were on the run. Hiding out somewhere to make a break for it as soon as the coast was clear. He was confident he would get her back in short order. That was his specialty. Jorge had bought off enough people in customs and immigration and even at the police headquarters that if news came in about Sunny and Billie, they'd know about it soon after. Pablo made some phone calls before he talked to Jorge.

"*Patron*, I have good news. I know where Sunny is

going. Many solid leads are coming in from the plants in police headquarters," Pablo said proudly as he burst into Jorge's living room.

Jorge was sitting on the couch, staring at an *I Love Lucy* rerun on the television screen, sucking on raw oysters, and chasing them down with a shot of Don Julio Gold tequila. The room was an unkempt disaster. A royal pigsty with empty beer cans and tequila bottles littered about. A full ashtray of overflowing cigarette butts sitting on the coffee table juxtaposed to a bottle of Pepto Bismal and an empty Twinkie box. The smell of stale, stagnant smoke and stinky, dead fish basked in a wet, fruity-air odor that permeated throughout the room.

To Pablo's surprise, Jorge was outraged when he realized Pablo failed to bring Sunny back to him. Jorge had been waiting, actually expecting Pablo to pull Sunny in behind him kicking and screaming. She was not there. The oysters were a waste of time.

"I warned you, Pablo," Jorge said, then spit in an empty oyster shell.

"Now she is gone to me forever. I heard she was fucking that convict and running off to Central America, isn't that right, Pablo? I am always two steps ahead of your sorry ass," Jorge lashed out.

"I will find her and bring her back to you, *Patron*. I promise. I beg of you," Pablo said, pleading for mercy.

"Come sit down next to me, Pablo," Jorge said in a quiet, menacing tone.

Pablo didn't move.

"Come here, sit!" Jorge demanded.

"Yes, *Patron*. I am sorry."

Jorge put his arm around Pablo's shoulder. "Why do you make me do this, Pablo?" Jorge said as he took Pablo by the throat with both hands.

"Please *Patron*, don't do this," Pablo cried through strained vocal cords.

"You had your chance, Pablo. I don't want that damn whore any more, anyway. She doesn't mean a goddamn thing to me now. I will find her myself. There is no need for you to worry your pissy little head anymore. My Sunny has been violated by another man. For that she must die." Jorge squeezed tighter; the jugular vein in his neck was popping out. Pablo's eyes burst wide open in fear. "This Billie Jensen man of hers will die right after watching me kill her. Slowly, painfully they will die…for no one crosses me, El Sanguinio. No one will have her now that she has been spoiled. You let me down, Pablo," Jorge screamed through clinched teeth.

Pablo wrestled free from Jorge's grasp. He ran for the door, ran for his life.

Jorge instantly grabbed Pablo by the back of his neck and threw him to the floor. He pounced on Pablo's back pressing him into the cold, damp cement floor. Jorge reached into the left side of his boot while he held Pablo's head down with his other hand. He pulled out his hunting knife.

Jorge jabbed his twelve-inch, serrated hunting knife all the way up the back of Pablo's spine. Pablo looked up at Jorge one last time in disbelief. Jorge felt a peaceful resolve as he slowly pulled the knife out of Pablo's back. He wiped it clean on Pablo's shirt and put it back in his boot.

"The bitch will get hers. No one will have her but me. I am El Sanguinio, right, Pablo?" Jorge said as he watched the dark pool of blood spread out from Pablo's body.

CHAPTER FIFTEEN

BLOW BABY BLOW

The Port of Beaumont
Beaumont, Texas

On the pier in Beaumont, Suneda, Billie, and Negos could hear the police sirens approaching from a distance and closing in fast.

"Hurry, you two," Negos insisted as he boosted Suneda up to the top of the cargo container. He pulled himself to the top and reached down for Billie.

"Billie, where are you going?" Negos asked.

"Just a minute, Negos, I need to create a diversion."

"What kind of diversion? There isn't time, Billie. We have to go," Negos insisted.

"We have to make time, Negos. In prison I bunked with an inmate named Andy Tasker. He's like a brother to me. When I told him of my escape plans, he agreed to help us. I contacted him when Suneda told me about you and your boat. He is supposed to have left a radio with a frequency activation trigger and an explosive device at the end of pier eight, under the last pylon on the left. He was released three weeks before I escaped. He promised to help."

"Hurry up then, Billie. They are closing in really fast," Suneda said.

Billie ran over to the pier where Andy was to have placed the radio and a bomb.

Detectives Morris and Logan were speeding to the Port of Beaumont from the tip received from Joe and Beth Sullivan.

"I hope those two cheesers from Wisconsin haven't put us on a wild goose chase," Logan said as he and Detective Morris entered the main port gate with lights flashing and sirens screaming.

"Even though they were a bit quirky they seemed sure of themselves."

Detective Logan slammed the brakes stopping their vehicle in its tracks. "Look at all these fucking piers, all these cargo ships to check out. How the hell are we going to find them?" Danny shouted.

"One at a time. We search them one at a time. Call for backup," Jackie said.

As Logan was panning up and down the sides of each of the twelve piers, he heard Negos start up the dual diesel engines that powered his cargo vessel. It was the loud churn of the motors and the deep bubbling sound of water thrashing under the aft that gained his attention.

"Morris, pier ten, where that ship just started."

Negos knew he had to bluff it by staying calm, devise a plan quickly and convincingly or the gig would be up as Detectives Logan and Morris approached the Pura Vida— the name on the side of the boat—and walked over the gangplank.

"It's Detectives Logan and Morris, Texas Rangers," Logan said as he and Morris flashed their badges. Negos was sitting in his captain's chair.

"Shut your engines down now and step back. Put your arms up where we can see them," Danny ordered while drawing his weapon.

"No, no *hablo* English," Negos said spitting out broken English and Spanish.

"Arms up. Stand up and move back," Danny repeated, this time with a hand waving gesture with his pistol in an attempt to get Negos to comply.

"*Si, Si,*" Negos said nervously. As he stood up from his seat, he put his arms up high.

Detective Logan bent over to turn the key counter clockwise to shut the engines down. Detective Morris raised her firearm toward Negos to protect Logan's flank.

"Have you seen a young man with a young woman around here? He is about six feet two with baby blue eyes and a buzz cut. There is a tattoo on his forearm of a snake curled around a heart with the word 'Mother' written underneath."

Negos just stared at Logan but he kept going. "The woman is about five feet with a dark complexion and long black hair. You wouldn't miss her. They might have been driving a blue sedan…"

Negos stood silent, thinking about his next move.

"Well, did you see them or not?" Detective Logan asked. He was getting irritated.

"No *hablo* English, *policia*," Negos said while shaking his head.

Putting his hands on his eyes and then over his ears and finally to his mouth, he replied, "No see, no hear, no say no nothing, *policia*."

Danny waved him off like he was some kind of a bumbling, worthless idiot.

"Logan, we are wasting our time here with this mute," Jackie said. "I'll check the boat over. You go back over to pier eleven and check the tanker that just docked."

"All right, but don't let this bumbler leave until I give the all clear, okay Morris?" Danny said.

"You're such a jerk-off sometimes, Logan."

Detective Morris scanned the port side of Negos' boat, then began a systematic walk around all of the neatly stacked rows of containers starting at the aft. She returned to the pilothouse to check the papers on the ships log, studying the materials and destinations manifest.

"Captain, I need you to open the shipping containers," Detective Morris said.

Negos' stomach tightened. He wondered what to do next.

"No *hablo* English, *Policia, no es comprendo*," Negos said once again.

"Let's start with that one over there," Detective Jackie Morris said as she pointed at the exact container Suneda had gotten into earlier. "Here on the log its container 12858."

"*Unos, dos, ocho, cinco, ocho, comprendo?*" Detective Morris repeated the number in Spanish as she showed Negos the log entry.

"*Si,*" Negos said, knowing full well he had to comply. He hesitated, then started walking toward the container.

"Hurry up now, Captain, it's getting late. I have to check them all before nightfall" Jackie said, clearly agitated. She waved her hands in a hurry up fashion to try and speed him along.

Suneda saw Detective Morris and Negos approaching her hiding spot through a small rusted crack in a hole the size of a nickel in the side wall of the container. She quickly opened the container and climbed down to the deck. She stood between two of the other metal containers, feeling completely trapped. Looking behind her, Suneda finally saw a tow line on the port side, about ten meters away that was dangling free from one of the ship anchor moorings into the water. Making a dash for it a split second before Detective Morris and Negos turned the corner and came toward her, Suneda grabbed the rope and shimmied down into the icy cold water. She held on for dear life as the ship swayed back and forth, occasionally pinning the dock bumpers and pushing up against the large wooden pylons. Freezing, shaking, and thinking she might get crushed against the pier, Suneda closed her eyes.

Help me, Sibo, Suneda prayed. Directly above she could hear their voices.

"Open it up. *Ahora*, right now!" Detective Morris said while pointing up.

Negos pulled out a ladder and took his time climbing up. Detective Morris was right behind him, nudging Negos up to move quicker, finally passing him as they reached the top of the container. She opened the container door and took a look inside. Nothing was out of the ordinary. Sniffing the aroma, the container was filled with twenty-five-pound bags of coffee beans stacked neatly on top of each other. The smell was captivating, enticingly exotic as it wafted up and through Morris' nose. Negos had retrofitted the container with a false back. In front were the coffee beans in neatly stacked rows, behind the trap door was a makeshift hide-a-way, living quarters he made specifically for Suneda and Billie's escape.

Seeing the detectives heading towards Negos ship, Billie knew he was running out of time. Bent in a crouch, he picked up his pace to reach the last pylon on pier eight. He knelt down, reached under the lip of the dock, and felt around. Sure enough, the radio transmitter was right where Andy said it would be.

"Christ, I hope I don't blow off my fingers with this thing," Billie mused. Hesitating for a moment, he finally pushed the "send" button and immediately there was a fiery explosion a quarter of a mile to the south at pier four.

"Damn it, damn it, damn it, I love Uncle Andy," Billie said out loud. He thought about the day he started calling him Uncle. An inmate had said something bad about Billie's mother and before Billie could react, Andy had the asshole pinned on the floor in a headlock, crying like a baby. Andy was one little bad-ass at five feet three inches and one hundred forty pounds.

"What did you say about his mother, you shit head?" Billie remembered Andy saying to the guy while he was choking the life out of him. He only let the dude up when the guards pounced on him and pulled him away. He earned the nickname Uncle Andy that day.

The three backup police cruisers that were dispatched to the scene to help in the search turned south back towards the explosion. Detective Morris and Detective Logan looked up from what they were doing.

"Holy crap," Jackie said as she shoved the ship's log back at Negos and jumped off his boat in the direction of the explosion. Logan was already on his way.

As she was running to catch up behind Logan, Detective Morris yelled out to Negos that he was free to push off. Negos nodded and waved back at her. He cranked up the twin motors, leaving them in neutral while he hurriedly moved around the boat to release the tie downs and mooring anchors one by one. He backed the Pura Vida off the dock.

"You're letting the stupid Mexican leave?" Logan asked as they ran along together.

"Nothing there, Logan. I checked the log and one of the containers. Best to let him clear out of the way so we can check the rest of the ships. It's getting late anyway. I have no plans to spend the night out here, especially with you."

Fearing a slowdown of his departure would get the attention of the police, Negos had no choice, he proceeded to turn the ship directly out, facing the open seas.

Seeing his ride on the move, Billie dove off the dock and swam to the ship, climbing up the same rope Suneda had been dangling from earlier. He climbed up to the shipping container and looked inside.

"Where is Suneda?" Billie shouted in Negos' direction.

The police on the scene determined the explosion on pier four was caused by an over-charged battery that overheated from an aging tugboat tied to the dock, setting off a stack of diesel fuel cans. Half the pier was engulfed in flames by the time fire fighters arrived to extinguish the mess.

Detectives Morris and Logan quickly searched the rest of the piers and cargo ships anchored along the port. By nightfall they came up empty-handed.

"You better call Tanner and let him know we got nothing here," Logan said.

"Yeah, yeah, Logan. You know he ain't gonna like hearing it. I'll call him when I get back in town. I can't take his bullshit right now. I've got a goddamn headache already," Jackie replied as she turned the cruiser left out of the Beaumont pier, heading west on Highway 105 back to Houston.

"Better you than me," Danny said as he slid his seat back, dropped his head on the headrest, and closed his eyes. Detective Morris looked over at him and punched him on his shoulder.

"You are such an ass."

"My ass is your ass anytime, Jackie."

CHAPTER SIXTEEN

BRAINFART

Detective Morris woke up suddenly from a deep sleep. She couldn't believe her mistake. The bumbling idiot on the first boat at the pier in Beaumont was from Costa Rica. She remembered the ship was flying an odd-looking flag. It had blue and white stripes with a red band and a military insignia in the middle. The name on the boat was Pura Vida. The container was full of coffee and should've been coming in, not going out.

"Holy crap, how did I miss that? What a brain fart. I saw it on Suneda Ortega's deportation order." Jackie reached for the phone and dialed her partner.

"Logan, it's Morris here."

"Yeah, I know it's you, sweetheart. What's up

Morris? It's three in the morning for Christ's sake. Have you been thinking about me, girl?"

"Yeah, in your wildest wet dreams, you prick. Hey, listen up for a minute. Do you remember that Mexican bumbler on pier ten you were so damned fond of?"

"The one you let go?"

"Well, I think that guy must be working with or maybe even helping Suneda Ortega and Billie Jensen."

Danny sat up. "No shit, what do you mean, Morris? It's too early to shake this hard on off."

"Wake up and keep both of your hands on the receiver, cockhead. Stay on point with me here. The ship was flying a Costa Rican flag. The name of the vessel was the Pura Vida. Do you get that detective dick? "

"Holy shit, I don't believe it. Great job, Morris!"

"Okay then, call the Coast Guard. Tell them to meet us at the main port in San Jose. Let's bring them in and get Stackhouse off your tight, squeaking little ass," Detective Logan shot back.

"Call them yourself," Jackie said and hung up.

✦

Billie opened the coffee bean door hatch and helped Suneda climb in. They were both exhausted and soaking wet. The makeshift "hotel room" with blow up air mattress was a blessing. The container was well equipped. The ventilation ducts Negos installed kept the internal area cool with a steady flow of air. The ice chest was loaded with beer, water, soft drinks, and fresh pineapple and mango juice. Negos thought of everything it seemed including flashlights, walkie-talkies, books, and magazines. It even had a port-o-john.

"Can you feel that, Billie? We're moving," Suneda whispered.

"Negos has come through just like you said he would. This place is nice. We could just stay and live here," Billie joked.

Simultaneously laughing, they rolled onto the quilt-topped air mattress. Slowly and methodically, without a word, Billie undressed Suneda. As the last button surrendered itself, her camisole slipped off, cascading to the floor below. Billie caressed her heavenly, light-brown breasts of pure silk and honey as he looked into her seductive brown eyes. He kissed her and stroked her now short brown hair, then his meandering lips made their way behind the ear and below her neckline. His mouth reached her large and supple breasts, taking one in as he firmly massaged the other. Without hesitation Billie moved on top of her. Suneda felt his thickened hard anticipation as he powerfully thrust himself deeply inside. Rolling his hips back and forth, in and out, Billie gazed into Suneda's waiting smile. Responding in kind to the pleasures of Billie's rhythm, in finely tuned concert with the rocking and swaying of the ship, Suneda came in waves upon waves.

"I love you, Suneda. I really love you. You are my angel from God above," Billie whispered.

"I know, Billie. I love you more. Sibo only knows how much," Suneda said.

They rested for a while, holding each other close, but Suneda was eager and quickly ready to explore more. Billie was sleepily convinced.

"Let's do that again, lover boy," Suneda teased, touching Billie in all the right places.

When they awoke in the morning, Suneda was feeling ill. The constant rolling of the small cargo vessel as it banged up against the twenty-foot swells made her stomach feel uneasy.

"You need fresh air, my love. I will signal out to Negos to see if the coast is clear to open the container," Billie said.

"Thank you, my sweet," Suneda responded, holding her tummy.

Billie picked up the walkie-talkie. "Negos, Billie here, over…Suneda is feeling seasick, over…"

"Sit tight, Billie. We may have a problem. Stay quiet, over…"

✦

With Governor Todd Branson's blessing, Captain Tanner dispatched Detectives Logan and Morris to catch the next flight out San Jose, Costa Rica. The media was in a feeding frenzy after word leaked out about the escapee heading for Central America. The story splashed out on the front page.

"Killer Escapee Eludes Police Net, Heads to the Jungles of Central America with Texas Rangers in Hot Pursuit."

Governor Branson's earlier attempt to put a lid on the story came loose at every end. His office was being bombarded with calls from concerned citizens and at the same time his opponents were calling for him to step down, saying he was weak on crime.

"Jesus Christ, Tanner, they're accusing me of being asleep at the wheel and that early voting this go round should send me packing. Can you believe this shit! Who in the hell do they think they are? Take care of this, will you." Governor Branson tossed the Houston Post on the sofa.

✧

Jorge had picked up on the news too. He found out who the two Texas Ranger agents were that were assigned to the case. Pablo had confirmed this news on his deathbed, too.

"I'll show them hot pursuit," Jorge smirked as he folded his newspaper into three perfect folds, putting it down neatly on the coffee table next to a pile of dried-out oyster shells. Getting up, he went into the bathroom to take a cold shower before heading to the Houston International Airport.

⟡

Logan and Morris boarded Pan American flight 308 to San Jose.

"Are you sure you want to bring Billie Jensen back, Logan, considering everything he's been through? I looked into his past after what Doctor Scott told us. The judge that sealed his records remembered little Billie. You remember Judge Plank, right? He told me Billie's nut job stepfather had molested other little boys. The bastard would seduce single mothers by wining and dining them for a few months before proposing marriage. He hoodwinked them into thinking he would be a good father and role model for their sons. Being husbandless with a child, especially in the 1950s, they were vulnerable for the lies and deceit, hook, line, and sinker. The sleazy rat would reel them in and eventually run off with their kid, just like he did with Billie. He was a goddamn Howdy Doody ice cream man, for God's sake. Sorry about my language but that sick-as-shit pedophile pisses me off," Jackie said after she gurgled downed her double Crown Royal.

"Look Morris, we have a job to do. Billie Jensen was convicted and sentenced for what he did. It's not up to us to let him go. We'll bring him back as we are told, hopefully alive, and the powers to be can sort all this shit out," Danny said.

"I guess you're right, but it still doesn't feel right. It doesn't seem fair. There is more to this story if you'd ever open up a bit and listen."

"Life isn't always fair, Morris. Time to put your big girl pants on."

Jackie held up her empty glass to the stewardess to get her attention.

"When we get to San Jose, says here in the dossier that we'll be meeting with a bounty hunter named Babu. Let's focus on that, Morris. This baboon guy will take us into the interior if we can't find them in San Jose. We'll go in and get out of there as quick as we can with Billie Jensen dead or alive."

The stewardess took Jackie's glass and noticed the man behind her had his glass raised as well. "I'll be right back, sir," she said.

Jorge nodded and smiled behind his dark glasses. Jorge's ears had perked up when he heard Babu's name. Babu worked for him when he needed a reliable tracker. On occasion Babu was hired to track down disloyal, thieving cartel members or anyone else that stole from him. To avoid detection while keeping the authorities guessing and one step behind him, Jorge built a spider web network of hidden drug routes throughout Central America. When one of his routes was breeched by a rival drug cartel or if federal authorities started sniffing around,

Jorge would unleash the unscrupulous police, politicians, and guerilla militia contacts he had in his back pocket. They loved the greasy money he lined their pockets with.

He remembered the time Babu brought him back a chicken thief. The poor Mexican was screaming and digging his heels in the dirt as Babu dragged and tossed him at Jorge's feet. Jorge pulled out a meat cleaver and quickly removed the man's hand and tossed it into a pig's pen where it was gobbled up as the Mexican cried and wet his pants.

Nobody steals from El Sanguinio. Billie Jensen took my Sunny. He will pay. No worries, he will be dead, Jorge thought as he envisioned cutting Billie's balls off.

"Here's your drink, sir, tequila on the rocks," the stewardess said with a smile.

Jorge nodded and smiled. He closed his eyes, intent on listening in for the duration of the flight.

✦

"Says here in the report, Suneda is a Boruca Indian. The Boruca live high up in the Talamanca Mountains in a place called Alta Vista. They exist as hunters and gatherers. Does this Babu fellow know the area and how to find where these reclusive people live?" Jackie asked.

"We'll see, Morris. That's supposed to be his job. Are you ready for a great adventure into the wild and crazy jungles with all its swampy, slimy creatures?"

"You know I don't like spiders and snakes."

"What about crocodiles? I hear they are BIG and plentiful down there." With a wide-eyed grin, Logan stretched his arms out as far as he could. "Ten to twenty feet in length, I'll bet."

"All right already. I am creeped out enough over this assignment without the bugs and lizards." Detective Morris sighed.

CHAPTER SEVENTEEN

SAY UNCLE

The Gulf of Mexico

B illie and Suneda crouched fearfully in the corner of the container, away from the hatch. It was difficult to keep upright in the swaying ship. Not knowing what was going on or what to expect, they listened intently for any clue.

They heard some feet shuffling and muffled voices. Then it was dead silent.

"I am scared, Billie," Suneda whispered.

"Quiet, baby, I think I hear something."

"This is the Coast Guard. We are going to board the vessel," a man with a deep, amplified voice announced.

After a few minutes, they heard an engine pull up next to the boat.

"Do you hear those muffled voices? Someone else is on the ship," Billie said.

"Oh my God, Billie, what are we going to do?"

"We sit tight just like Negos said. They won't find us in here if we stay quiet."

Billie and Suneda didn't say another word. Suddenly, they heard the door to their container squeal open. Billie put a finger on his lips.

The secret hatch opened, letting in the light of day. Billie rose to a fighting stance, resolved to fight for their freedom or die doing it.

When his eyes finally adjusted to the bright sun, he saw a man standing in front of him and he leaped for him, pressing him against the side of the container. "I am going to kill you, Uncle Andy. You scared the living crap out of us, man. You're an asshole," Billie shrieked and grabbed Andy around the neck to pull him into a hug.

"And I see you have just the shitter in there to take care of it for me," he said, laughing, "Quite a place you have here."

"That's enough, you two boys, I need some fresh air," Suneda said as she crawled out of their hiding place. "Shall I close the hatch or do you two want to be alone?" Suneda said.

Once on deck, the three of them gathered around and hugged. Negos quickly joined the reunion.

"So this is Suneda. I can see why you kept her hidden.

She's a real gem. You're in over your head, man," Andy told Billie.

"Yeah, he knows," Suneda giggled. Then she lost her smile as she grabbed hold of Andy's thick arm.

"Thanks for being here, Andy…Really, thank you from the bottom of my heart."

"No problem, little lady. I'd give my life for that boy of yours," Andy said

"Me too, Uncle Andy," Suneda said.

Billie looked at her and smiled, obvious adoration in his eyes.

Negos went back to his captain's quarters at the stern of the ship and returned with four glasses and a bottle of twelve-year-old Ron Centurion rum.

"A toast to the great escape, may we live to be free one more day?" Negos toasted the fellowship of his family and new-found friend.

"Here, here, to the good life, *pura vida*! To Alta Vista," Negos said.

"To Alta Vista," they said together, raising their glasses high up to the morning sun as it was breaking over the eastern horizon.

⚜

Negos stayed twenty miles off the Texas coastline heading south in the Gulf of Mexico. The next morning, Negos gave Andy the wheel as he went aft to clean up the deck from their impromptu celebration the day before.

When he turned to head back to the cabin, he looked up and stopped in his tracks. The Costa Rican flag was flapping in the breeze. A feeling of anxiety instantly crashed in on him as he tried to remember if the police noticed his flag, especially the red-headed detective. Did that woman police officer see it, he wondered. No way, he reasoned. Otherwise, she would have taken us down right then and there.

Negos was visibly shaken. Deep down he knew their cover was blown, and he was the one who blew it. It would only be a matter of time before the real Coast Guard showed up.

"What will I tell them?" he said to himself.

Suneda came up from the galley to wish Negos a good morning with a cup of dark-roasted coffee in her hand.

"*Buenos dias*, Negos, *es café con leche*," she said, handing him the cup.

"*Buenos dias, bonita* Suneda. *Muchas gracias*," Negos replied, forcing himself to smile.

"*Con mucho gusto*," Suneda acknowledged, reminiscing the times she and Negos would have their morning *café, huevos*, gallo pintos, and *plátanos* for breakfast back in their village.

"*Si*," Negos said quietly, remembering those times too.

"What's the matter, Negos, you look like you've seen a ghost. Casper the friendly ghost, I hope," Suneda said with a chuckle.

Negos hesitated. "Oh, my Suneda, I may have tipped

the police off. The Costa Rican flag has been flying since we left the Beaumont dock," Negos replied almost crying. Admitting failure was hard for him.

"Negos, we have to tell Billie and Andy right away. I am glad you told me sooner rather than later," Suneda said.

"I am sorry, my little niece. I am a stupid Boruca. I have ruined everything for you and Billie. I spoil everything for anyone I am with," Negos said, his voice cracking.

"No worries, Negos, really, no worries. I know Billie, he will figure something out. He always does." Suneda attempted to calm him.

Suneda and Negos approached Billie and Andy to explain the situation. They all agreed they could not take the risk of hoping none of the authorities noticed the flag. Together they came up with a contingency plan. Rather than disembarking in the Port of Limon in San Jose, as originally scheduled, Negos charted a course toward Hopkins Village, Belize. There was a man there named Horace who owed him a tremendous favor. It was time for Negos to call it in. Billie, Suneda, and Andy would get off at the mouth of the Sittee River, to meet up with Horace. He would guide them into the interior rain forest, escorting them through the jungle until they would rendezvous with Negos at the bridge at Alta Vista. Negos would continue as a decoy on to the Port of Limon and act as if nothing was amiss. He would record his log and tell the authorities his run to New Orleans was abandoned because of bad weather. If anyone tried to follow him, he would shake them off, and hike in to the rendezvous spot at the bridge.

Negos pulled the cargo ship up to the dock in Hopkins Village in Belize. A man waving wildly greeted them upon their arrival as if they just finished a race. Negos had radioed Horace as soon as they had decided on their new plan. As requested Horace brought with him backpacks, sleeping bags, tents, food, water, machetes, and two inflatable rafts.

Horace lived in a small cabin on the Sittee River that ran east and west through central Belize and emptied into the warm, blue waters of the Caribbean south of the village. Horace worked as a river guide, fur trapper, and trader. Born a Canadian citizen who migrated to Costa Rica, Horace moved with his family when he was a boy.

Over the years, now and then Negos would stop by to visit Horace during his cargo runs to Houston. It was a midway stopover point for him to get his land legs back. Besides, Horace could cook up some really good Belizean-style Cajun grub full of jalapeño peppers that were hotter than hell. They were Negos' favorite.

Horace carried supplies up and down the banks of the rivers, selling them at remote villages all the way to Honduras. Bringing blankets, socks, boots, and dried beef in trade for mustelid furs and crocodile hides, which brought him a handsome sum. Everyone in the rain forest knew of Horace. He stood six foot five with a balding head that sat on a pencil-thin frame. He was a weathered fellow of sixty years with skin as tough as iguana lizard leather and the inside of a wandering soul. He was known by the locals as the "Walking Stick Man."

Horace hugged Negos as he stood on the dock.

"My friend, what do I owe you for your presence here? I owe you my life, Negos. What do you ask of me?" Horace told Negos this on every visit, wanting to repay his debt.

"No worries. You owe me nothing, my friend. I know you would do the same for me. These people are my family who just want to go home. Can you take them there safely, protect them along their journey as if they are one with me? This is all I ask," Negos said.

"Your wish is my command, Negos. I will protect them with my life as you have with mine. Come with me, my new friends." Horace reached out for Suneda's hand and pulled her from the ship to the dock. Billie and Andy stepped up behind them.

They would stay in Hopkins Village for the night, get some rest, and head out at daybreak.

"Soon we will be together again, my dear friends. Meet me at the bridge at Big Fork, just outside of Alta Vista," Negos shouted from the bow of his boat. He threw off the tow lines and headed south towards the Costa Rican Port of Limon.

"Where is the bridge at Big Fork?" Andy asked.

"It is the last fork in the Rio Saverge, just before you cross over to Alta Vista, the village where I am from," Suneda responded proudly.

"That is near where I met your Uncle Negos. My horse was struck by a viper snake and died there. It threw me and I busted my leg in three places. See the scars right here?" Horace showed them two distinct gashes where bones once protruded from his leg, now covered up with aging scar tissue.

"He carried me all the way to the Port of Viejo, almost breaking his back. I would have died had he not come along that day. He is my guardian angel."

"How many days will it take to travel there?" Billie asked.

"It should take seven or eight nights through some very rugged terrain. I have mapped a course for us. We will head south down the Mosquito Coast, along the beach until we reach Honduras. This will take three days. From there we will hike it through Nicaragua, then another week to the Costa Rican border."

"Just a stroll along the beach, I love it," Andy howled.

"Andy, this is serious shit. We could die out here," Billie said.

"Just lightening things up here a bit, Billie boy," Andy replied.

"Stop it you two," Suneda said sternly. For a small person, she had a commanding voice when she needed to.

"We need to all work together. We have a long road ahead of us. Agreed?" Horace added.

"Yes, agreed," they all said.

"Once we reach Nicaragua, we will hike into the interior for one day until we reach the Coco River. From there we raft to the Rio Saverge split and take that until we reach the bridge at Alta Vista. The rapids will move us along quickly. That's where we'll meet up with Negos.

They each picked up as much gear as they could and followed Horace down the beach. Minutes turned to hours and hours turned to days. The group plowed ahead, keeping small talk to a minimum. The heat, humidity, and bugs were enough to deal with.

They stopped for lunch on the second day. "We should reach the Coco River by nightfall. We'll get some rest soon," Horace said in a tired voice. The climate didn't bother Horace but the walking did. He was used to traveling by boat.

At that moment, a cloud above them burst open. Rain started pelting down. It was thick as the flow over a waterfall. They hurriedly and clumsily pitched the two tents and climbed in to wait the storm out. Andy and Horace were bunkmates in one of the tents, and Suneda and Billie were bunkmates in the other. Billie, Andy, and Suneda eventually fell fast asleep while Horace kept watch. There were many hungry predators that came out at night in the rain forest, searching for food. Jaguar, puma, and ocelots forever roamed the jungle, stalking prey and ready at any minute to leap at the first sign of a tasty meal.

Billie was about to fall asleep when he heard a most startling sound.

"What the hell is that?" Billie cried out. He sat up as quickly as he could while shielding Suneda with his left arm, a machete in his right.

"Oh, Billie those are just howler monkeys. You have lots to learn, my big bad jungle man," Suneda said, pushing him back down. "Howler monkeys travel in families of eight to twelve females with one male leading the pack. They travel in wide circles, foraging and gathering food. When the alpha male is ready to move on, he starts a howling grunt sound to get everyone's attention. When the females are ready to move, they grunt back to let him know they heard him," she explained.

"They sound like a big ass-kicking gorilla to me," Billie said as he loosened his grip on the machete.

"Yes, they do, but believe it or not, they are only twenty-four to thirty inches tall."

"I don't think I could handle that many females," Billie joked, pulling Suneda in close. "I feel sorry for the poor little monkey-man. I can barely get you to do as I say."

Suneda looked at him sharply. "Just like sometimes I can't get you to do what you say you'll do, Billie."

Billie rolled over, knowing better than to start an argument with a very stubborn woman.

CHAPTER EIGHTEEN

OUT IN THE BLUE

South of British Honduras
Caribbean Sea

Several hours passed by from when Negos dropped Billie, Suneda, and Andy off in Hopkins Village. He was full steam ahead into the Caribbean Sea as he left the Gulf of Mexico behind. Off in the distance a boat was fast approaching, lights flashing as it pulled up next to Negos' vessel.

"This is the Coast Guard. May we have permission to board your vessel, Captain?" Lieutenant Mark Casey said over a speaker in an authoritative voice.

"*Si*, permission to come aboard." Negos rolled his

arms in circles inward welcoming Lieutenant Casey and his three sailors on deck while sporting a shit-eating grin on his face. Lieutenant Casey noticed this facial expression immediately, but decided he was being a sarcastic ass who probably didn't like authority figures. He had seen it many times. No one liked the Coast Guard unless they were in trouble. They had to succumb to his requests, and he enjoyed the power play.

Knowing the trio were no longer on the ship and every trace of them had been removed, Negos felt a sense of control over the situation. He thought he would play it coy and ride it out.

"We're looking for two escapees from Texas known to be on this ship. Stand down and let us search your vessel," Lieutenant Casey demanded.

Without hesitation, Negos let them pass by to do their work. They scoured the vessel for thirty minutes, only to come up empty-handed.

"No one else is on board, Lieutenant Casey."

"That's convenient, isn't it, Captain? What is your name? Where are you from?" Lieutenant Casey asked.

"I am Negos Ortega from the province of Puntarenas, Costa Rica," Negos stated proudly.

"What is your business out here with empty cargo containers?" Lieutenant Casey inquired.

"I unloaded my goods in Beaumont. Teak wood, bamboo, coffee, and chocolate were my cargo. I was to bring a load of steel and plastics back from the Port of

New Orleans, but they canceled the run because of bad weather on that side of the Gulf," Negos said.

"That's right, Lieutenant. The ships manifest shows a New Orleans run that was shut down because of Tropical Storm Betsy," Staff Sergeant Bobby Higgins reported.

Negos looked to the sky and thanked Sibo.

Lieutenant Casey knew he was had, but he had no proof. Shaking his head in bewilderment, he had to release Negos and his vessel.

✦

"What do you mean they were not on the ship?" Detective Logan said as he answered Lieutenant Casey's call in the telephone booth at the airport in San Jose. He and Detective Morris had landed thirty minutes earlier and were waiting on Casey's report.

Jorge was listening in on the conversation from around the corner.

"That's right. We checked out everything. No one was onboard except the Captain. I thought that was strange so I put a tail on him. Ships manifest says he's headed for the Port of Limon. We'll follow him there, make sure he gets off alone. You and Morris should head over to the port and follow him from there. If he heads into the interior, I am pretty sure he'll take you to the people you're looking for," Lieutenant Casey said.

"Good thinking, Lieutenant. Do you know where

he could have ditched the convict and his girlfriend?" Logan asked.

"It had to be somewhere along the British Honduras coast, maybe Plancencia, or Dangria. I have a detail circling back to check it out. We'll coast into and out of a few of the docks and interior shipping lanes along the way and report back to you stat," the Lieutenant said.

"Sounds like a plan. Keep us informed. We need to report back to Stackass, I mean Stackhouse, at 01100 hours."

"Roger that, Detective."

The detectives headed to baggage claim, watching for Babu so he could escort them to wherever they needed to go.

Babu had been waiting at the airport for the arrival of the two detectives, watching them as they moved through the concourse.

Babu was a tall black man whose complexion was dark as coal. He stood sturdy at six foot tall, sporting curly dreadlocks that shimmered in the sunlight. He was an attractive, formidable sight. His forearms were thick as tree trunks. His legs were like logs. He seemed to be of Jamaican decent. Possibly from the Caribbean side of the country. Babu by his nature was as instinctive a tracker as a puma on the hunt. For the right price, he could find anyone or anything. He had an uncanny nose for it.

He waited about a half an hour before approaching and introducing himself to Detectives Morris and Logan.

His father always told him to be patient, observe all of your surroundings first before proceeding into any kind of situation or confrontation to ensure it was what it seemed or was supposed to be. The coast seemed clear enough.

"Hey mon. Yous twos Logans and Morrises?" Babu asked in his Belizean accent, a broken dialect prevalent in the Caribbean side of the country. For extra assurance he raised a homemade sign above his head with the words "Lowgans ans Morress" poorly written.

"Yous, I mean, you Babu?" Detective Morris said, correcting herself.

"Yez, dat meez, mon. Ats yer senorita's services."

"Nice to meet you, Babu. I'm Jackie Morris" Jackie said, sticking out her hand. Babu took it tentatively." This is Detective Danny Logan." She pointed to her partner, who gave him a relaxed salute. "Can you take us to the Port of Limon first? We have to check out a ship that should be docking there in a couple of hours."

"No problems. Meez froms dems parts, mon. Knows'em likes de backs ofs meezs hands. Meez takes yous dere, now."

"Lead the way then. We are in a bit of a hurry," Danny said.

Babu was directing the detectives out of the airport when he saw Jorge lurking in the shadows. His defense mechanisms shot way up. His hair was standing up all over his body, but his survival instincts told him to keep still and be quiet.

What's El Sanguinio doins heres? Babu thought as he lifted Detective Morris' duffle bag over his shoulder and grabbed Detective Logan's pack.

"You okay, Babu?" Danny noticed his distracted manner as they exited the airport out into the humid air.

"Yez, me alrighties. No worries, mon. Let's gets toos. Nights soons toos come," Babu said as he gathered his composure.

With their gear in hand, Babu escorted them through the dusty parking lot to a white 1962 Jeep Wrangler 4X4 with no top or doors. Babu packed the detective's bags in the back, opened the door for Morris, and waited for Logan to get in, then jumped in the driver seat to fire the vehicle up. As he looked into the rearview mirror and pulled out onto Highway 1, toward San Ramon, he noticed Jorge was tracking right behind them in a camouflaged Land Rover, a jaguar on the hunt.

Babu kept what he knew to himself, not wanting the detectives to suspect anything. He had to figure out what was going on first. Jorge seldom did his own dirty work, ordering it done by his lackeys instead of dirtying his own hands. The fact that Jorge had arrived unannounced and was stalking them himself concerned Babu, big time.

Did Jorge want these two detectives for something? Did they cross him? Did they owe him something? Were they on the take? Was there something on that ship coming in that Jorge wanted: drugs, women, money, or all of those? Babu didn't have any answers. He had to stay on high alert and ready himself for anything. Did Jorge want him dead? No, he didn't think so; Jorge used his services often. *But one can never be certain about these things*, Babu thought, remembering what his father always told him.

✦

Taking his time so as not to appear to be in any rush, Negos continued on his schedule after the Coast Guard vacated his boat. He pulled into his slip at the Port of Limon. Nothing seemed out of the ordinary. Ships were coming in and going out as normal. Crews were loading and unloading their cargo just like any other Saturday. It was the normal hustle and bustle of a busy port city.

Negos tied up his boat to the anchor moorings, then proceeded below deck to gather his belongings.

Of course, Negos' old hunter and survival instinct told him to be on the lookout for anything suspicious. But he didn't notice anything out of the ordinary.

Negos packed his bedroll, a change of clothing, and a duffle bag with enough food and water to last for seven days. He would hunt and forage for what he needed after the rations were gone. As per the plan, he would rendezvous with Billie, Suneda, Andy, and Horace at the bridge at Alta Vista the following Saturday. Even though Negos made this journey before, he had to get moving before dark, knowing seven days was a push. It was a long and treacherous way through unforgiving and unrelenting territory. He had his machete by his side with a filet knife tucked away in his right boot. One never knew what might be around the next bend or hiding behind a boulder or a tree.

Seemingly, the coast was clear as he walked down the dock towards dry land.

"*Hola*, Negos sir." A local dock hand approached the boat waving. "How was your trip?"

"It was good, Julio. It was very good."

"Would you like me to swab the deck and close her up for the night?" Julio asked.

"*Si, amigos*, I am going to see my *familia*, Julio. I will return in two weeks. Keep an eye on my boat. You can stay on for security and sleep here until I return, if you like. I will pay you when I get back."

"*Gracias*. Did you see my friend Horace this trip?" Julio asked, happy to accept the offer. Julio had trapped with Horace many times and they had become good friends.

"*Si*, he is as ornery a goat as ever, meaner than a hungry mustelid," Negos chuckled as he walked away, not wanting to engage in small talk or anything that could slow him down from his mission.

The Jeep Wrangler turned onto the road in front of the port as Negos entered the jungle on a well-worn path across from the port entrance. Babu pulled into the port parking area and they all three got out. On the way to the port, Jackie had told Babu who they were looking for. From the Coast Guard description, they knew what Negos' boat looked like and they had all seen it docked at the pier. Babu knew of Negos but had never met him. Babu started for the boat.

"Where are you going, Babu?" Danny whispered.

"Dat mon, Julios," he said pointing to a man on the deck of Negos' boat. "Me talks toos him, seez wherez es Negos and wherez he be goins."

"Then hurry up, Babu, we need to find out where he is," Jackie said.

Babu jumped up on the dock and headed towards Negos' slip.

Julio was clasping the windows shut in the pilothouse when Babu approached him.

"*Hola*, Julie. Wherez Negos?" Babu asked as Julio bent down to secure the tie downs to the anchor moorings.

"He went to see his family," Julio explained.

"Ins Alta Vistas?"

"*Si*, Alta Vista?"

"Wherez he comin' froms?"

"Hopkins Village."

"No one elses wiz him now?" Babu asked.

"He came in alone. Why do you ask?"

"Jus es wonderin's, es all," Babu replied. "When he leaves?"

"*Cinco minutos antes*," he said holding up five fingers.

"*Gracias*. Later, mon." Babu walked back to the Wrangler and the two anxious detectives.

"So what'd you find out," Danny said.

"He goins toos Alta Vistas. Just leaves. Dere," Babu said, pointing to the path across from the entrance to the port.

"Well, let's get going then. We have to follow him," Jackie said, stepping up to get in the jeep.

Babu grasped her arm. "No drives. Long walks, nines, tens days. Weez needs suppliez."

"Shit," Danny said and leaned against the side of the jeep.

"We don't have any choice, Logan. He's got to be meeting up with Billie and his girlfriend so we have to follow him."

"I knows toos Alta Vistas. Me follows, no problems. Suppliez first."

Jorge had driven past the port entrance and parked. He watched from a distance, sitting in the Land Rover as Babu and the detectives got in the jeep and left the port.

"Where the fuck is my Sunny and her soon to be dead lover boy?" Jorge pondered as he got out of the 4X4, slamming the door shut. He walked up to Julio, who was mopping the boat's deck. Jorge walked up from behind and tapped him on his shoulder.

Startled, Julio dropped the mop. He turned abruptly about face as he stood staring directly into El Sanguinio's stoic, red eyes. His jaw opened up wide exposing his tonsils and several missing teeth.

"Oh it's you, *El Patron*," Julio said, obvious fear in his voice.

"Where is that fuck going?" Jorge demanded.

"Who's that fuck?" Julio asked, shaking.

"You know who the fuck I'm talking about: Babu," Jorge yelled back, reaching out and grabbing Julio by his throat.

"Babu was looking for Negos. Wondering where the fuck he was going. He's going to Alta Vista."

"Who in the fuck is Negos?" Jorge asked.

"He owns this boat. I am watching it until he returns."

"Where are the others?" Jorge said, gesturing to the boat.

"There were no others, boss."

"Where the hell are the rest of them? This Negos must have told you something. Where did he drop them off? Think, you dumb ass, think," Jorge screamed.

Julio was trying to think. "Ah…Hopkins Village that's what he told me, *Patron*, he came in from Hopkins Village, that's where," Julio replied proudly.

"Now that wasn't that hard was it, my man Julio?" Jorge said, calmly patting him on the head.

Julio was screaming as he hit the water twelve feet below. He immediately surfaced and treaded water, waiting for Jorge to leave.

"A good snitch's life is worth keeping. Can't have enough good snitches 'cause the dead ones don't do much good." Jorge thought how logical and clever he was.

"Get back up here, you dumb fuck," Jorge yelled at him.

Julio swam back to the boat and climbed back up on the deck with the rope Jorge threw down to him.

"Release the ties and push us off."

Julio, dripping wet, did as he was told.

Jorge jumped into the captain's seat of the Pura Vida and fired up the twin turbos.

"Where are we going, *Patron*?' Julio asked as Jorge backed the boat out of its slip. That last thing he wanted to do was head out into the middle of the sea with El Sanguinio.

"Hopkins Village, dumb ass, where else? Now go make me something to eat."

Julio complied.

✦

At daybreak, Suneda, Billie, Andy, and Horace continued heading south along the Mosquito Coast. The first few days were behind them. After the torrential rain the night before, it was miserably hot and even more humid and now the breeze had evaporated under the scorching sun. The sweat poured off them in beads the size of raindrops. Mosquitoes were as big as houseflies. Flies as large as hummingbirds or at least that is how it seemed to Andy and Billie.

"Three days of this shit and I'll be as skinny as him." Andy pointed up ahead at Horace.

Horace dismissed him with a wave of his hand. He was in no mood for Andy the smart ass.

The hike along the coastline was dangerous for them. Being out in the open most of the daytime exposed them to searching eyes. They knew the Coast Guard probably would be out looking for them. Any signs of a boat approaching the shoreline in their direction caused them to scatter into the jungle and wait it out for the coast to clear, making for a painstakingly slow, miserable journey.

At the end of day three they pitched their tents just inside the tree line of the beach for the night. They had a half day of travel along the coast left before heading due south, directly into the interior, towards Nicaragua.

CHAPTER NINETEEN

CAT AND MICE

Elana packed a bag for travel. The more she thought about it, the more she just could not believe the miraculous turn of events unfolding in her favor in every single way. She had her trip all planned out.

With a little help and some luck, she knew she would see Billie again. Detective Morris told her he was alive and she was going to make sure he stayed that way. Doctor Scott confirmed he was doing all right, too. Her motherly protection instincts would not fail her this time. As long as she had her way, never again would Billie ever be alone or feel alone.

On her way to the airport, Elana wondered what Billie looked like as a full-grown man. *Did he look like his father? Was he tall? Did his hair color darken? Did he have his father's personality? Did he know his life's secret?* She smiled as she nestled back in her seat in the plane to take a quick nap.

It will be good to see him and hold him again. We have so much to catch up on. I have to trust Detective Morris and Doctor Scott, she thought as she drifted off to sleep.

The plane touched down at approximately10:05 a.m., jolting Elana awake. Grabbing her carry-on bag, Elana exited the plane and headed for immigration. With all her documents in order, she breezed through customs and hailed a taxi.

"Take me to the Sisters of Charity mission," Elana instructed the driver.

"*Si, Senorita.*"

It will be good to see the mission again. I'll grab a chopper flight with them to Alta Vista. Elana was so excited.

✦

"Mister Detectives Logans, sir, can yous tells me why weez be trackin' Negos?" Babu asked.

"We're following Negos because he is aiding the escape of a felony convict from Texas. He is with his girlfriend, too. We suspect he's meeting up with them, probably in Alta Vista. We are going to follow him there and bring them all back to Texas to face charges," Danny said.

"Can you take us there ahead of them?" Jackie asked.

"Me cans. Me knows dese'em jungles like me backs of me hands.

"Do you know Negos?" Detective Morris asked.

"Yeez, mon, me knows Negos, mon."

"We don't want Negos, Babu. We only want him to take us to find the escapee from Texas," Danny insisted.

"Just bring us to Alta Vista. That's all we ask. We'll take it from there," Jackie said.

After they had been on the path a while, it became thick with vines and low hanging branches, muffling any low sounds and light, protecting their cover. Babu, Jackie, and Danny had to cut their way through the thicket with machetes. It was a slow, arduous but steady process, taking one step, one bladed whack at a time. The noise of the cicada's mass droning was deafening at times. From the moment the sun rose until dusk passed to nightfall, the cicada's thundering hum electrified the rain forest and all but drove them crazy. The three hikers could barely hear each other speak. It was almost unbearable to even think as they trudged on in silence, unable to avoid the nuisance until at last it was night.

"There must be over a million of those creepy, noisy bugs," Danny shouted from the back of their single file line.

"That's probably a good thing. No one wants to hear you anyway," Jackie shouted back

"Ha, ha. Those buggers are driving me insane!" he said.

"You're already crazy, Logan, no worries for you," she said.

"Dems cicadas. Dey comes up froms buried deeps belows ground onces each years for twos weeks soes dey can mates. Den dems retreats belows," Babu explained.

"Their probably getting more than I've gotten in the last ten years," Danny yelled out.

Jackie and Babu burst out laughing at Danny's expense.

Babu continued to take the lead, following a safe distance behind Negos. It was a methodically slow and tedious dredge through the thickness with machete's clashing back and forth, whipping at small branches and leaves. The insects were large and nasty looking. The flora and fauna were robust, displaying a multitude of colors with tantalizing fragrances wafting from all directions: a hummingbird paradise.

As they entered a clearing, Danny stomped on a spike-haired, long-legged spider the size of a tea cup saucer.

"That'll teach you, you big ugly bastard. This place gives me the creeps," Danny said as he peeled the dead arachnid off his shoe with the blade of his machete.

"Lets keeps movin'. Da sun soons toos sets. Dems cicadas rests for da nights, danks toos Sibo," Babu said

The sixth night was fast approaching. The cicadas quieted down to a deafening silence.

"I can't hear you" Danny said jokingly.

"Times toos sets up camp. Tomorra weez be reachin'

dese Coco Rios." Babu put his pack down on a large boulder near a small creek. The other hikers were still ten meters behind him working to catch up.

"Shhhh…" Babu said when he realized the cicada's had stopped their noise making before the sun had set.

He put his pointer finger across his lips. The wind seemed to pick up the tree limbs to bow slightly. They were all aware of a strange stillness around them and put everyone on high alert.

"Somethin's not right. Dems cicadas, nevers dems stops a chirpin' tils completely darkens."

"I don't hear or see anything, nothing at all," Jackie said in a whisper.

"What's wrong up there?" Danny wanted to know.

"Gets yer machetes, Master Logans, and yous, Misez Morrises, stayz behind me." Babu dropped the pack off his back.

An instant later, a shadowy figure came out of nowhere, stalking with its steely black eyes and flaring nostrils as it moved closer in to its prey. Confident in its stealth, the creature pounced on Babu's back, catching him completely off guard. Dazed and confused, Babu reached for the knife he had tucked away in his belt but he was too slow. The puma bit deep into his shoulder, ripping off his arm as Babu screamed in pain. He fell to the ground, bleeding profusely. He saw Jackie and Danny approaching but he could not hold on. When Danny finally reached him, Babu's eyelids closed, never to open up again.

It was then that they saw the big cat. The puma turned to look at them and snarled as if they were there to steal its prey. Jackie and Danny moved slowly back. Proving his authority, the cat seized Babu by the neck, sinking its teeth in, then ferociously shaking him back and forth to dislodge Babu's head from his body. The sound of bones crushing and flesh ripping left indelible marks in their minds.

Danny, shaking at the ghastly sight and haunting sounds, pushed Jackie back and raised his machete over his head. He screamed like a madman and ran at the puma. The big cat grasped Babu's head in its mouth and ran, quickly engulfed by the jungle.

"Holy shit, Holy shit, that thing just killed Babu. Holy crap, holy shit what the hell was that?" Jackie yelled, running up to Danny's side.

It was dusk now. Visibility was getting poor. The streaks of light shining through the canopy were dimming. With no more than twenty minutes of daylight left, the detectives were scrambling to get a grip on what just happened.

Jackie began to cry and then she bent over and retched.

The cicadas started buzzing again. A low humming at first, then steadily increasing in decibels until the multitude joined in full concert.

Danny put his arm around her. "Anyone of us could have been attacked by that thing, it just happened Babu was in the front of the line," Danny said in a daze.

Morris started trembling and shaking, so Danny pulled her in close.

"We need to set up camp here for the night, whether we like it or not. I'm not leaving until I can see what the hell is in front of me," Logan said.

"Yes, I agree, but we can't lose sight of Negos. He's our only way out of this now. Once we find him again, we'll pitch the tents and build a fire around us to keep that thing away."

"Yeah buddy. No problem. I'll take the first watch. I can't sleep right now, anyway. Did you hear that you little fuckers? Go to sleep you bastards," Danny yelled at the cicadas.

Almost on command, the cicadas slowed their haunting song. Silence drifted into the jungle as a drizzling rain commenced, then stopped as suddenly as it began.

Negos witnessed the puma ripping his friend Babu to pieces when he circled back after he heard him scream. He listened in on the detectives' conversation from a thicket of teak trees and could tell they were clearly in over their heads. Negos could hear the fear in their voices as they decided what to do next. He felt sorry for the gringos, even though he knew they must have been following him.

"This is scaring the shit out of me," Jackie said, pointing her gun out into the dusk, blinking at the darkening shadows.

"This is fucking with my head too, Jackie. Pick up your gear and follow me," Danny said.

"What are we going to do with...what's left of Babu?" Jackie asked.

"We can't help him now. We need to make camp and get a fire going before that thing returns."

Detective Morris followed her partner's instruction as they gingerly moved out from the dense foliage into an opening that appeared to be an abandoned village of some kind. They stopped when they spotted the smoke and flames of a small fire in the distance. They retreated back into the jungle until they could no longer see the village and they set up their own camp.

Logan took up the first lookout position. Digging a small trench by hand to form a circle, he placed dry logs and branches in the ditch that surrounded their tents and lit them on fire. The two of them sat back to back facing the fire in opposite directions. The warmth was comforting. While Morris tried to get some sleep, Logan was on full alert, gun in one hand—safety off—knife in the other, machete lying next to him.

✦

In a small clearing cut out from the brushy thicket, Billie, Suneda, Andy, and Horace unpacked their gear to pitch their tents. With a couple of hours of daylight left, there was plenty of time to relax and set up camp for the night.

"I'll go get some dry wood to build a fire," Horace said as Billie and Andy raised their tents. Suneda rolled up a couple of logs to sit on and cleared out an area in the middle for the fire pit. When she was finished, she sat on one of the logs and stared at the empty pit. Billie sat down next to her.

"I'll go find some wood too," Andy said and walked off to let them be by themselves.

"We are halfway there, princess. Only a few days left to go," Billie said while rubbing the top of Suneda's leg.

"I am so happy, Billie. I can't wait for you to meet my family." Suneda put her arm around Billie.

As Horace walked off a good distance away, he sensed something was rapidly closing in from behind. Instinctively he turned around, wielding his machete. In one full circle the machete whizzed over Jorge's head, missing him with only an inch to spare. Jorge ducked under the swing.

"What the hell are you doing out here in the middle of nowhere. Who in the hell are you? I thought you were a jaguar sneaking up behind me." Horace said, trying to explain himself to the stranger.

Jorge grabbed Horace with one of his thick paws and pushed him up against a tree. Staring at him with black, glowing eyes, Horace could see pure evil. The guy was powerful, as strong a man as he had ever encountered. Shaken but not afraid, Horace stood patiently, preparing for his next move. He had learned much through his years as a trader, living alone out in the wilderness most of his life.

"You'll die unless you tell me what I want to know. Do you understand me?" Jorge said with a vice grip clamped around Horace's neck.

"Yes, I understand you, Horace said in a strained but calm voice. Who the hell are you, anyway?"

"El Sanguinio, that's who. Ever hear of me?" Jorge replied grinning.

"Can't say that I have," Horace replied, gasping for a bit of some air.

"You'll find out soon enough."

"What the hell does that mean?"

Jorge didn't reply, he just glared at Horace. He was surprised this man did not know who he was.

"What are you doing out here in the middle of nowhere?" Horace asked.

"Trying to find my girlfriend"

"Your girlfriend? You mean Suneda?" Horace asked beginning to put two and two together.

"You got it, smart guy."

"How the hell did you find us out here?" Horace said, wondering what the hell was going on. They were almost to Nicaragua for heaven's sake.

"Your big-mouth friends in Hopkin's Village pointed me in your direction. You left a trail as wide as an elephant. Even a blind monkey could find you," Jorge said proudly

"What do you want from me?" Horace asked.

"Not a damn thing. I just simply need you out of the fucking way," Jorge said. Then he pressed one hand over Horace's mouth while trying to snap his neck with the other. Horace struggled frantically against Jorge's thick forearm. He was able to kick him in the nuts and dart off into the rain forest.

"I am going to kill you, you fuckin' pencil-neck," Jorge squealed when he was finally able to run after him, dodging protruding branches.

Horace ducked behind a rock formation as Jorge ran by, holding his balls. Jorge continued his rampage for another thirty meters then stopped dead in his tracks. Out of breath, he needed a break and time to think his options through.

Horace stayed as quiet as he could. Not knowing who or what the hell else was out there, Horace decided that strangling this maniac with a vine would be his best option. A stabbing would cause quite a ruckus, something Horace didn't want anyone, including Billie, Suneda, or Andy to hear. He did not want to alarm them until he knew what he was dealing with, and he did not want to put them in harm's way. He had made a promise to Negos and he planned on keeping it.

Jorge was sitting with his back perched up against a banyan tree, sucking the juices from a tamarind fruit as he continued his lookout for any sign of Horace. The tamarind was bittersweet. He tossed the rind away and smacked his lips. Jorge enjoyed this type of cat and mouse game. He was the cat, as always.

As he was about to get up, Jorge felt something crawling up his leg. He looked down and there was a banana spider about the size of an avocado pit with long, black hairy legs and two sharp fangs. Jorge flinched when he first saw the ugly creature and then smiled when he recognized what it was.

"Oh, no you don't, little feller," Jorge said as he picked it up by the back of its neck. It struggled to gain a foothold onto anything it could.

Uhmm…not your day is it, my little friend?" Jorge then proceeded to put the hairy spider into his mouth. It made a crunchy squishy sound as he chewed. Just the way he liked them.

"*Muy bien*. I needed another snack before dinner. I need protein," Jorge said as he belched out loud. He then pulled out two of its legs that were lodged between his teeth.

Horace shook his head, disgusted by what he had just seen.

When Jorge stood, Horace lassoed the vine around Jorge's neck, pulling it together with all the strength he could muster. Bucking, clawing, and swinging his hips wildly in an attempt to free himself, Jorge put his fingers under the tightening grip of the vine. Horace struggled to hold his ground. Jorge was a good half a foot taller and had at least fifty pounds on him. Horace's feet slipped underneath him and threw him off balance, losing the advantage he once had. In a judo move, Jorge pulled Horace over his back and down to the ground in front of him. The vine released and they wrestled in the dirt.

"The cat always gets the mouse. Such a little squiggly rodent, thinking you could kill the great Jorge! You should know better, boy. You are no match for El Sanguinio. No one is, my poor, little squeaky friend. Your time has come and gone," Jorge said with a blood-lusting grin.

Jorge sat up on top of Horace, pummeling his face unmercifully with his massive fists. Horace, clearly no match for Jorge's strength, fell unconscious. Jorge pulled out the long hunting blade he had sheathed in his waistband and quickly carved a deep line across Horace's neck, severing his jugular vein. Horace quivered, choked, and shook violently on the ground as he bled out.

"Did you hear that, Billie? I mean did you notice how still it is just now?" Suneda asked.

"Yes, that the strangest thing. I guess I should say the strangest feeling I've ever had," Billie said.

Andy dropped the wood in his arms. "Everything went silent for like, thirty seconds. How weird, man, then poof, everything back to normal, just like that." Andy snapped his thumb and middle fingers together.

"Where's Horace? We need to find Horace," Suneda said.

"I'll go take a look. He headed out that way," Andy said as he pointed towards a cluster of banana trees.

Jorge dragged Horace's limp body into a thicket of thorny vines, then buried him in a compost of fallen leaves, twigs, and branches.

"Horace, is that you? What's going on?" Andy asked as he came towards them. Jorge slipped into the shadows and backed away into the dense foliage.

Andy saw Horace's feet. "Horace what happened,

man?" Andy shouted as he ran the last few meters. He pulled the debris off of him.

Andy went to check the pulse in Horace's neck but saw the gaping wound and knew he was dead. "Billie, Suneda!" Andy yelled. "Come quick!"

Billie and Suneda raced over to him.

"What happened to Horace, Andy?" Billie asked.

"I don't know. I found him lying here all crumpled up with his throat slit. The dude's gone; he bled out," Andy replied.

CHAPTER TWENTY

C'EST LA VIE

Captain Tanner was summoned to Governor Branson's office for a chat about the case. When he entered the room, Branson was leaning back in his leather swivel chair, legs perched up on his mahogany desk, clipping his fingernails. He sat up when Tanner entered the room.

"Well, have they found Billie Jensen yet?" the governor asked.

"Not yet, boss, but they are hot on his trail somewhere inside Costa Rica. We received a transmit signal," Captain Tanner said.

"What exactly does that mean? You promised me, Eddie. A transmit signal? You either have him or you don't. Don't waste my time here. What else are you NOT doing to secure this mission?" Branson said, not wanting a sugar-coated answer.

Captain Tanner sighed. "I guess I'll have to head down there to do the job myself," he replied.

"You guessed right, Edward. It's about time you stepped up to the plate. This is getting way out of hand. The media is all over this thing. They are telling the public that poor Billie Jensen was being dorked big time by his stepfather, for Christ's sake; that's why he killed him. I know I would have snuffed his ass out if it were me. Did you know about this? Public opinion is going soft on me, saying I'm not up for the job. I'm slipping in the polls, falling fast. Who the fuck leaked the story, anyway?" the Governor asked, demanding Tanner's full attention.

"The records were sealed, Governor."

"Bullshit. I could have used this tear-drop story to cover my ass. I could have been in front of this fuckup, not behind it."

"I'll round up a posse of senior dicks to take with me and we'll take the next flight to San Jose. I'll have his sorry ass back by midnight, dead or alive." Captain Tanner gave Branson a two-finger salute.

"Jesus, Tanner, you have to bring him back alive, for Christ sake. Haven't you heard anything I just said? Am I going to have to take care of this myself?" Branson howled.

"We'll bring him back alive, Governor."

"Just get the hell out of here and do your job," Branson said, dismissing him with a wave of his hand. Then he went back to clipping his nails.

＋

Detective Morris rose from her watch position against Danny, waking him out of his sleep. It was daybreak at last. Her back and shoulders ached from trying to sleep upright with one eye open most of the night. The fire had died out a couple of hours ago with only a few embers still smoking. Her morning breath was not appealing. An empty gnawing feeling in her belly required foraging for something to eat. Jackie found some yucca root close by and quickly began eating it to fill her stomach.

Danny had fallen back asleep. "Wake up, Logan, it's morning. We have to get moving to keep up with Negos." Jackie handed some yucca out to him.

"We have to bury Babu first," Danny insisted as he eagerly accepted Jackie's offering of food. Jackie nodded in agreement.

They gathered rocks and stones and covered Babu in a rock coffin, then offered up a brief prayer before picking up their packs and heading south toward Negos and the Coco River.

Every step they took they kept an eye out for danger. The thoughts of last night's horror kept them both on high alert. Danny had Babu's machete in hand to cut through the vines and his gun ready to ward off any possible threat. Jackie kept her eyes wide open, sweeping her head back and forth and occasionally looking back over her shoulder, the gun in her side holster unsnapped.

"Negos can't be too far ahead. See that smoke diminishing into the clouds up ahead. You can smell it too. That must be him," Logan said while sniffing the air. "It's almost like he's letting us find him."

"You think so, Logan? Why would he do that?"

"Maybe it's a trap."

"I don't know. It doesn't make sense. Why wouldn't he just leave us lost out here, to fend for ourselves and starve or let us get eaten up by something big and nasty?" Jackie questioned.

"All I know is we better keep up with him or your thinking might come true."

Silently, Morris and Logan plowed forward, looking for any signs of Negos.

"We should be getting close to the river Babu was telling us about. He said when we see the mountain formation that looks like a camel's back, we would be close," Danny said.

"See over there? I think that's it. Look, Morris, it's right over there," Danny said as he pointed south, excited about the find.

"That means we are only halfway there," Jackie, the usual optimist, said with a sigh.

"We only have halfway to go," Danny, the usual pessimist, replied.

The closer they got to the river, the more difficult the terrain was to navigate. And the farther they moved into the interior, the more alive the rain forest became. Different species of colorful birds crisscrossed in front of them, singing the praises of a beautiful day. Blue morph and zebra longwing butterflies were fluttering their colorful wings as spider monkeys climbed high above them, swinging and playing in the tree canopy. The croaking sound of bullfrogs signaled they were close to water. Two scarlet macaws took flight and startled them as the two approached an opening to the Coco River.

"Finally, we made it to the river. I never thought I would be this happy in the middle of nowhere," Danny said.

"No doubt about it Danny, my boy," Jackie said as she let out a sigh of relief. She rolled her backpack off her shoulders and leaned against a wall of rock. The sound of water crashing below made it hard to hear.

"Look ahead there, Morris. Negos is setting camp up across from us up on the left, about two hundred meters down," Danny said as he pointed downstream.

"Lay low, Logan. Don't let him see you. We need to make a larger clearing and set up camp for the night too. We still have three more days to go, according to what Babu told us," she said with a forced smile. She was trying to show she was glad they made it to this point. Deep down, she was afraid of what may lay ahead for them.

The two novice campers once again unpacked their bedrolls and packs, and flipped up the two tents.

Although the skies were clearing up for the night, there was a chill in the air from a recent downpour. They decided to chance a small fire to keep warm and hopefully cook some food.

Danny made a couple of fishing poles out of bamboo stalks. By fastening one of their ropes to one end and using one of Jackie's hair pins at the other, he formed a workable pole and hook.

Jackie dug up some grubs and earthworms for bait. Within thirty minutes, Danny caught enough fish to stuff them full, cooking them on the open fire pit.

"I don't think these trout ever had filet mignon ala earthworm," Danny said as he served himself.

"I am glad they were so hungry because I am starving. Let's eat," Jackie said.

Once they had their fill of trout they felt drowsy. They knew Negos was clearly not going anywhere any-time soon; he had some laundry hanging out to dry over a makeshift line.

"I am going to take a walk to clear my head. Keep an eye on Negos. Don't let him out of sight. I'll be back shortly," Jackie said as she pulled out her gun and headed back to where they came in from.

"Ten four, boss. Over and out," Danny said not paying much attention except thinking about getting a nap in. Then his stomach growled.

✦

Billie, Suneda, and Andy were shocked by Horace's death. They were puzzled as to what could have happened to him, but finally realized they were in grave danger.

"Someone killed Horace. No doubt about it. I've been in lots of fights in my time and he was beaten without any mercy before they sliced his throat. He didn't stand a chance, man," Andy said, shaking his head.

"You're right, Andy, just look at his face. It looks like he was in a boxing match with a goddamn gorilla," Billie said as he studied Horace's disfigured body.

"Not to mention his throat being slit," Andy said.

"Why would they try and bury him?" Suneda asked.

"To try and hide his body, let us think he ran off or something," Andy replied.

"Billie, I am not feeling well," Suneda said as she crouched over.

"What's the matter, Suneda?" Billie asked.

"I am so scared. I think Jorge killed Horace. He's probably lurking nearby. I just know it. I can feel it. I can smell it," Suneda said. She started to shake.

Billie held her tight in his arms.

"Let's grab our gear and get the fuck out of here," Andy responded.

Suneda looked down at Horace. "Shouldn't we bury him or something?"

"We don't have time, Suneda. Whoever did this is

still out there. We need to get going. Try to put some distance between him and us," Billie said.

Suneda started to cry. Billie took her by the hand and led her back to their camp.

Horace had drawn up a shortcut for them the night before, shortening the trip to the bridge at Big Fork by a full day. The trio grabbed Horace's map, what gear and food of his they could carry and set off.

"Stay together, keep alert. If it is Jorge, I don't think he'll try and jump the three of us. We'll deal with him soon enough, I'm sure," Billie said.

Jorge was right behind them, staying back just within earshot. He couldn't wait to get his "loving hands" on "his" beautiful Sunny. Having just satisfied his craving to kill, Jorge felt invincible. It gave him power. He needed more.

It's the cat now against the three scared, blind mice, Jorge thought. Once he got their little friend out of the way, he would let Sunny watch him painfully kill her boyfriend and then take her life slowly after sexually torturing her. It would be merciless, pure unadulterated fun, and he waited patiently for the time to make his move.

Billie, Suneda, and Andy hurriedly followed the map, which took them along a narrow path high above the raging Coco River below. They needed to get to a spot along the river that was navigable before they made the final leg of the trip on the river itself.

"According to the map, we cross Windy Bridge up there," Andy said, pointing above them, map in hand. "Then scale down the path to get down to the river."

The trio entered the wood-slated bridge as it swayed back and forth as if mocking the ravaging currents below. While fighting the wind gusts in their faces, they took one steady step at a time, holding onto a tethered rope that traversed the length of the bridge.

As soon as they reached the middle, Jorge charged at them from out of nowhere, catching them off guard.

"Oh my Sibo, it's Jorge. He's coming for us! Billie, do something!" Suneda screamed.

Billie and Andy turned around to confront him.

Jorge advanced on them without hesitation, reaching Andy first. He quickly smacked Andy in the head with his bare hand, causing him to lose his balance and slip over the side of the bridge. Andy grabbed hold of a board on his way over, stopping his drop to the raging river below.

"Run to the other side, Suneda, run…cross the bridge and keep running. Don't look back," Billie yelled.

Suneda hesitated at first, then complied.

When Jorge reached Billie, he grabbed him around his neck with both of his hands, pressing his full weight on top of him. The two fell to the floor of the bridge with a crack. Jorge pulled Billie up by his shirt and kneed him in the groin. Billie fell back against the single-rope railing bouncing back towards Jorge. As Billie caught his breath, Jorge ripped out one of the rotted wood slats and charged at Billie.

Andy, still holding on for dear life, reached through the newly exposed opening and tripped Jorge as he went by. Stumbling to the edge, Jorge grabbed onto the rope railing and it snapped in two. He swung on the loose end with one hand for a moment, twisting in the wind, then he plunged down into the river below. Suneda stopped and turned around. She ran back to help Billie pull Andy back up onto the bridge.

Suneda looked down at the foaming water. "Do you think he's dead?" Suneda asked as Andy got to his feet.

"I don't know, man, but it was pretty cool watching him fly past me. You should have seen the look in his eyes. That could have been me," Andy replied, thinking the worst.

"No one could survive that fall. You're lucky to still be here, Andy," Billie said firmly.

"Amen, brother. We are all lucky to still be here," Andy said.

"El Sanguinio is dead? I can hardly believe it," Suneda said, still a bit skeptical.

Jorge hit the water belly first. The force of the fall knocked the wind out of him, putting him out cold. Floating and bobbing face down for several minutes, the river currents took him racing downstream. He finally settled in a swirling, six-inch deep pool, eventually floating him to the side of a sandy bank. Coughing up the muddied water as he gasped for air, Jorge spit out the remaining fluid in his lungs. He pulled himself up and sat in the shallow waters.

"I am El Sanguinio. I am truly invincible," Jorge said, spitting sand and debris from his mouth.

"Maybe I will throw her boyfriend off the bridge at Alta Vista. See how he flies," Jorge smirked.

CHAPTER TWENTY-ONE

SNAKES ALIVE!

Detective Logan had an armful of mango tucked under his chin as he walked back to the campsite. Jackie was not back yet. He cozied himself up against a small embankment under the mangrove trees that stretched out over the river. It was a serene, peaceful spot except the sun was piercing hot. Danny laid the fruit he collected out in a line to choose the ripest ones. Selecting a yellowish-orange one, he peeled the skin off with his pocketknife. It was sweet as honey, a succulent burst of flavor. The sticky juice trailed down his hand and dripped off his fingers. Danny reached up and snapped a tiny, leafless twig off a tree branch above him, to help dislodge a chunk of fruit that was wedged in his molars.

Satisfied with his sweet snack, Danny grabbed a large banana leaf and covered his face from the blistering sun that still managed to make it through the trees. He stretched and closed his eyes, ready for a short siesta.

Directly above him, perched in the mangrove branches, a boa constrictor curiously watched Danny as he drifted off to sleep. The snake was twenty-five feet long with the girth of a telephone pole. The snoring puzzled the snake, although not enough to stop his hunger; the last thing it ate was a small spider monkey about a week ago. With its split eyes focused and its tongue testing the scent in the air, the boa uncoiled gradually on its way down the trunk, inching closer and closer to Danny.

Danny rolled over, adjusting the large leaf on his head. When he moved, the boa stopped. The boa held back, unsure of its prey, waiting for the right moment. In a split second, the boa moved down on top of Danny, wrapping itself around his neck decisively and unmercifully.

Danny's dream girl ran off as he woke up, gasping for air. It took him a moment to figure out what was happening. First, he tried to pull the thing off his neck with his hands, but the creature kept squeezing and choking him. Frantically, patting around the ground with one of his hands, he tried to locate his knife but he couldn't find it. He tried to yell as he continued to pull at the thing but the beast was powerful and slimy, so he could not gain any leverage. Hopeless thoughts of his life ending raced through his mind, draining his will to fight. A last flash of light came in as total darkness fell in and he passed out.

Believing its prey was dead, no longer a threat, the boa loosened its grip. With victory seemingly in hand, the boa pulled Danny down to the riverbank and swam upstream to enjoy its dinner.

✦

Billie, Suneda, and Andy reached the other side of Windy Bridge, confident in the thought that Jorge was dead. They hiked down to the river below to scope out a resting place for that night.

They were a day ahead of schedule, flatout tired and completely exhausted from the day's events. They pitched their tents to take a much-needed siesta and called it a day. Later, after a simple meal of canned beef and hard bread, the three fell fast asleep in their tents.

Bang, bang your dead…the monsters dead, yeah, yeah the monster's dead. Bang, bang.

"Stop it. Stop it," Billie wailed out loud as he sat up swinging.

"Billie, it's me. Wake up, dear. It's okay. I am right here for you, sweetheart."

Andy woke up too, unzipped his tent and looked in Billie and Suneda's direction.

Suneda held Billie close. He was breathing heavy as though he had just finished a marathon. He was sweaty and sticky, just like all the other times.

"Easy, Billie," she whispered softly. "I hate this dream too."

"I'll never shake this nightmare, Suneda, never."

"Yes you will, Billie. It might take some time, but I know you will."

"I am okay now, my love. Thanks for being there for me, as always," Billie said calmly as the thoughts of the dream dissipated.

"You guys okay over there?" Andy yelled out as he stuck his head out from his tent.

Suneda unzipped her and Billie's tent flap. Billie clearly needed some fresh air.

"As soon as it gets light out, I think we should stay here the rest of the day and have some fun. What do you say guys? We are a day ahead of schedule anyway. We could go back over there to the waterfall, swim, and make the most of it," Suneda said, trying to lighten the mood.

"I like that idea. I could use a bath, anyway, to get this dreadful stink off," Andy said.

"Yeah, I was going to say something to you about that," Billie teased. "I'm just kidding. I smell bad like a polecat, too. You've come up with a groovy great idea, Suneda."

"And once you get rid of that polecat smell, I have a treat for you," Suneda told Billie.

"I like the thought of that even better. Let's go swimming," Billie said as he gave her a sly smile.

Andy rolled his eyes. *Damn she's a good looker. What I could do with that,* he thought.

"I'll let you two love birds have your time together. When it gets light out, I'll go get some firewood and look for some fruit and berries for when you return. Then I am going fishing," Andy said.

At daybreak Andy headed back down the trail they had come from yesterday, while Suneda and Billie ran over to the waterfall on the other side of the river. A pond of refreshingly cold water swirled underneath the descending water that streamed down from the mountain peaks. Billie pulled his shirt off, then stumbled around on one leg, awkwardly trying to remove his boots, pants, and underwear. Suneda followed his lead.

Billie beat her in, but Suneda dove in right behind him. The icy cold water tantalized their skin with an invigorating chill as they came up for air. They embraced and kissed as though it had been forever.

"I love you, Suneda."

"I love you more," Suneda said as she held on and gave him another long, passionate kiss. They made love.

"Harder, faster," Suneda moaned.

Billie complied.

Suneda squealed in pleasure as they both finally let go.

Billie and Suneda swam over to a nearby rock ledge, splashing at each other and laughing. They climbed up the steep embankment to catch the warmth of the sun as it came filtering in through the tree canopy.

"I think our lives our changing for the better. You make me feel alive," Suneda said as she lay down next to Billie.

"You make me want to live," Billie said, leaning over to kiss her.

She took him in her hand until he was hard again, then she rolled up on top of him.

Pleasantly surprised, Billie smiled.

Andy scurried up the steep embankment with his backpack to get a bird's eye view of the surrounding area, kicking stones back down on his way up. The face of the cliff was sheer as he approached the top. He climbed up by grabbing hold of protruding rocks, sticking his foot into crevices, and holding onto root masses, giving him leverage to lift and pull himself up. He figured the climb was a hundred feet up. The exercise felt good. More exhilarating than the drudge of walking all day. Standing tall on the plateau looking out, he could see the entire rain forest canopy stretching for miles and miles, rolling along in what looked like a manicured landscape. It was a beautiful vista. The sun was shining through the cloud cover. The river was raging down below. He could see rain falling a mile or so away. The treetops were glistening and a rainbow was beginning to take shape over him. Andy could smell the freshness in the air. He took a deep breath, taking in the serenity and majestic of the beautiful scene.

"Damn it, I should have brought Billie's Polaroid up

here. What a beautiful place this is. Beats the hell out of the pen."

Taking a seat on a fallen tree, Andy rifled through his pack, pulling out a book to read.

"You should have brought more than that," a voice said behind him.

"What the fuck…?" Andy looked up at the scratched but intact face of Jorge. "We thought you were dead man," Andy wailed.

"You are mistaken, my friend. I am El Sanguinio, the invincible," Jorge replied as he pulled his shirt up exposing his hairy, red chest.

"El Sanguinio, what the fuck is that? Speak English, man."

"El Sanguinio loves blood. I kill for pleasure. I kill for money. I kill for fun. You two boys have my girlfriend so I will kill you for vengeance, for my honor," Jorge boasted, then he pulled his knife from its leather case.

Andy reached for the blade he had tucked in his waistband, but Jorge shoved him to the ground near the cliff's edge first. He got back up on one knee, as small stones and dirt fell over the side.

"Stand down. I'm an Army Ranger" Andy said, his military training kicking in.

Jorge didn't listen to his seemingly futile command.

"And I am a drug lord. You are in no position to tell me what to do," Jorge chuckled.

"What do you want, man? Why don't you let us be? Suneda doesn't want anything to do with you."

"It doesn't matter what Sunny wants. It's what I want. I have a job to do and you are part of it."

"You're a fucking nut job," Andy yelled.

"Names will not hurt me. See no broken bones. But you will not be so lucky."

Jorge came at him with his knife.

Andy stood with his knife in hand but slipped on his loose footing. Jorge lunged and Andy dodged to get out of his way, slipping on the small stones and losing his balance. Jorge easily pushed him over the edge.

Andy fell rapidly. Glancing off the side of the cliff several times and bouncing off the rocks until he came to a stop at the bottom, about fifty feet from where Billie and Suneda were sitting.

"Andy! Oh my God! Andy, what happened?" Suneda screamed. "Are you all right?"

She knew this was a dumb question. It was obvious he wasn't. Andy's body was contorted in many places. There was blood and deep purple bruising up and down his torso, indicative of massive internal bleeding. The bone in his left leg was sticking out as it twisted back behind his shoulder. He was gurgling and mumbling incoherently. The top of his scalp was missing above his left ear.

"Holly shit! What the hell happened!" Billie yelled out confused as she stared at Andy's crumpled, listless body.

Andy did not move or speak. He made eye contact with Billie and was trying to tell him something. Billie leaned in but couldn't understand his jumbled words.

"What are you trying to say, Andy? Tell me. Did you slip and fall? Did you lose your grip? What the hell just happened?" Billie demanded. Crying, he picked up his friend by the shoulders and hugged and rocked him.

Andy tried blinking his eyes in Morris code; one, two, one, stop, one two one, one…, but neither Billie nor Suneda picked up on it. Suneda thought he was having a seizure.

Andy then lost consciousness. Suneda sat next to him and Billie in shock and disbelief. She tried to sort out what just happened.

Andy took a deep breath, gasping for air. He coughed up blood and then was still.

It doesn't make sense. Andy was a skilled climber. It was a hobby of his. Was this an animal of some kind or did he just slip and fall, or is someone else out there? Billie quizzed himself, trying to regain a grip on his usual self-confident composure.

Billie sat holding onto Andy for hours not wanting to let him go or believing he was gone. Suneda sat next to them in silence, letting him mourn the loss of his dear friend. She would always be there for Billie, always.

"We have to go, Billie. It's time," Suneda said in a motherly tone.

"Negos will be waiting for us at the bridge at Alta Vista."

Billie and Suneda buried Andy. One more day and they would be in Alta Vista.

✦

"Geez Louise. Where the hell are you? Do you hear me?" Jackie said muffling her voice through a hand-made mega phone. "Damn it, Logan you're supposed to be keeping your freakin' eyes on Negos.

"Come on, Logan? Quit fooling around. Where the hell are you?" she continued, making sure her voice would not carry over to Negos' camp.

Jackie strolled over to the mangroves where the ground was disturbed. Drag marks were visible from where she was standing all the way down to the river. Danny's coat was balled up in the dirt forming what looked like a pillow. Jackie noticed a sticky, gooey-like substance on the leaves and branches above. She pinched a wad of it off between her fingertips and rolled it around, then she smelled it.

How odd; must be some kind of sap.

She reached in Danny's side pocket for the transmitter radio to notify Captain Tanner that something else had gone wrong. She could feel it. It was broken, busted up from an obvious struggle, but with whom or with what? Jackie pulled her revolver from the holster.

"Damn you, Danny, for leaving me out here alone, damn you!" Jackie said under her breath.

The radio clicked on for a few seconds, made a couple of sounds and then turned off.

Jackie peered tentatively downstream. Negos was

breaking camp. Detective Morris had no choice. She had to follow and keep up with him or she would be stranded out in the middle of nowhere. They would never find her in time. She had few survival skills. If the animals didn't get her, she'd die of starvation or poisoned from eating something she shouldn't. If she made it out, she would come back to find Danny later.

Hiking along the winding river path was painstakingly slow. The moss on the rock beds was slippery. Invasive vines with sharp thorns intertwined with other fauna and hurt like hell when Jackie brushed past them, sticking into her skin and ripping flesh.

Occasionally, a welcoming cool breeze would drift down the mountain and meander its way upstream to give her some relief from the heat and soaking humidity. Jackie wiped the sweat off her forehead with her shirtsleeve.

"Watch your step, Grace," Jackie said to herself. Then a moment later she let out a bloodcurdling scream as she lost her footing and plunged down a steep embankment into the stream. Jackie sat in the cold stream and let the water move lazily around her.

"This place is a bitch." Jackie pushed wet bangs out of her face.

When she tried to stand, she clenched her teeth, grimacing in pain and reaching down for her ankle.

"I wish I could get this over with and go home. A jungle is no place for a lady."

"What the hell was that?" Negos quivered, pausing when he heard the high-pitched noise of a woman's scream.

"Stupid gringos, why don't they just go home and leave us alone," Negos sighed, then doubled back to check on the detectives.

"I am going to need to rest for a few minutes," she said, knowing every minute she sat, Negos would be that much farther ahead of her, and he was her only ticket out of this hell on earth.

Detective Morris hobbled her way over to a hilly knoll and plopped down. She held and massaged her ankle, trying to wring out the pain.

Jackie's ankle was swelling up to the size of a coconut. It hurt like hell. She could not put any weight on it at all. She knew she was in trouble. In frustration, she threw the transmitter radio up against the side of the riverbank where it shattered into multiple pieces. She cupped her hands over her face and began to cry.

A few moments later a figure moved upstream about fifty meters away, and it was coming towards her. Alarmed, Jackie pulled the revolver for its holster and pointed it in the direction of the approaching stranger.

"Who's there?" Detective Morris asked as soon as the figure was twenty meters away.

"Easy, Detective. Don't shoot me. I came back to help," Negos said.

I heard you scream so I came to help you," Negos explained. "Where is your partner?"

Jackie furrowed her brow. "How do you know I'm with someone?"

"I heard Babu scream and I came back. I saw the puma take his head away. Ever since I have been staying close so you don't get lost."

Jackie's brow furrow deepened. "Something or some-one took my partner, about fifty meters back that way." Jackie motioned behind them. "So now you can speak English? You played us like fools at the Port of Beaumont," Jackie said forcefully.

"I did what I had to do to save my family, Detective," Negos shot back.

"And who is this family you're referring to?" Jackie demanded answers as she tightened her grip on the pistol.

Negos deflected her question. "I thought it was just the two of you following me, so I circled back to come up behind you to see if you knew where you were going, then I found the body of my good friend Babu covered with rocks."

"So, after you found out Babu was dead, you were going to sneak up on Danny and me and kill us. Is that how it was going to go?" Jackie asked as she raised her gun ever so slightly, stiffening her wrist up and pointing it squarely at Negos forehead an arms-length away.

"No. No. No. I was going to get the two of you spun around, get you lost out here and then finish my business, figuring you would call for help from the local *policia*. They are good at finding lost tourists, especially gringos. Happens all the time," Negos explained as he put both of his hands out in front of his nose as if to deflect a bullet if one was going to come his way.

"What exactly is your business here, Negos? Give me one good reason why I should believe you and not just shoot you right here, right now."

Searching his mind to find a suitable answer to trick or deceive her was his natural inclination. Thinking twice, Negos decided to tell her the truth, the whole truth and nothing but the truth.

"Let's keep moving, and I'll tell you along the way," he said.

Jackie took in a deep breath. Now she knew she was alone. With Danny gone, Jackie decided she had to trust Negos. With a bad ankle, she was out of options.

Negos lifted Detective Morris' arm and put it around his shoulder. It was time to continue on the journey to the rendezvous point at Big Fork.

"I think your ankle is broken, Detective."

"It hurts like hell just to put a little weight on it," she admitted.

They traveled down the trail gingerly, watching each step so as not to trip on an exposed root or a slippery rock.

"You asked me what my business is out here, Detective."

"Yes. Why are you here, Negos?"

"I am helping my little cousin escape a bad life in

America. She was abducted by a drug lord the day she arrived in the United States. He used her as his prostitute and drug mule. Her life has been hell. She wants to come home. We are going home."

"How do you know Billie Jensen, then? Do you know he is an escaped convict? He was in prison for killing his stepfather and assaulting a fellow inmate."

"Yes, I know his story, Detective."

"Do you also know I'll need to bring you to face charges for aiding and abetting a criminal as well as obstruction of justice?" Jackie stated as a matter of fact.

"By chance or from the good grace of Sibo above, I was brought back into Suneda's life to bring her to safety back to her home, Detective. Do what you must do. If that is your justice, so be it. I will do what I must do to protect her and Billie," Negos said sternly.

Jackie thought deeply about what Negos just said. Having a soft spot in her heart already for Billie and now hearing about Suneda's story, it made her want to cry, but she didn't want to look weak in Negos' eyes.

"The night he abducted Suneda was horrific for her, he shot her up with a narcotic mixture, raped her in his van, tied her to a bed post in a sleazy, rat-infested hotel room and repeatedly had his way with her. He controlled her for two years, pumping her up with drugs and threatening her life if she ever tried to leave him. I will kill him," Negos explained.

"Holy Christ."

"Suneda told me that one day one of Jorge's capo's smiled at her and told her she was the most beautiful woman he had ever seen. Jorge overheard this comment and he immediately went crazy. He hit the guy in the back of the head with a baseball bat just hard enough to knock him out. When he awoke, Jorge had him tied to a train track. He brought Suneda with him to witness it. She begged him to release the man. She said she had never seen such a look of fear in someone's eyes. He cried and cried for mercy, actually shit his pants. Jorge just smirked and grinned as the sound of the train whistle got closer and closer. The train severed the poor man's head right off. El Sanguinio brought it back on a stick and placed it in the center of town," Negos said.

"Oh my God, how terrible. He is pure evil."

"Yes, he is evil, Detective. I would even say he is not even human."

"Billie and Suneda are in grave danger. If we know where they are headed, I'm sure Jorge knows as well," Jackie said.

Jackie winced as she bent over to feel her ankle. The swelling was intensifying. She started feeling cold.

"We'll rest here, Detective. I need to make you a walking stick and find some salve to rub on your ankle to reduce the swelling."

"Thank you, Negos."

"*Con mucho gusto*, Detective, it's my pleasure. Keep alert and have your gun ready."

He knew he had to do something quickly, before her body went into shock. He wasn't sure why he was helping the gringo, but he couldn't leave her alone in the jungle. He would figure out what to do with her once he met up with the others.

CHAPTER TWENTY-TWO

THE RUNAROUND

The boa had Danny coiled up in its tail section as it slowly meandered its way down the Coco River. Danny was still alive, but just barely. If the snake's hold wasn't enough, the river water choked him as he bobbed about trying to catch a little bit of the breath he had left in his lungs. Dazed and confused and really scared as hell, Danny realized it was a large snake that constricted his airflow. The snake had snapped his left knee and dislocated his right shoulder. Danny was a jumbled mess. The pain was excruciating, shooting out in every direction, although he knew it was wise to be silent. He watched the tree canopy high above in flickering shades of light and dark as he tried to figure out his next move. The snake slithered into a small cove cut out on the river's edge. Tall wetland grasses surrounded him. A couple of parrots took flight and an iguana ran for cover as the snake pulled its prey onto the shoreline. The boa released its grip and Danny recoiled in intense agony. The boa moved away seeming to take a step-back-look at his food. Danny saw this as his advantage to make his move. His left arm was the only chance he had; his right arm and shoulder were useless. He wiggled his body back around, using his right leg and foot to circle around to face the snake. Danny's movements seemed to catch the snake off guard. Danny could sense the boa didn't know what to do next. A stick or a rib bone from another feast jabbed Danny's side. More pain or dumb luck as would be. Danny reached under his side and was able to get a firm grasp on the object with his good hand.

"Ya took off a bit more than you could chew, big fella," Danny blurted out as he mustered up just enough strength to lunge at the snake and stick the rib bone into one of its eyes. The boa coiled back in complete surprise and retreated into the dense underbrush.

Danny rolled over on his back to get some temporary relief. Fresh air came rushing into his chest cavity, even though the exhalation would bring him to tears. Looking skyward, he could barely move. Besides bones broken, he was bleeding badly from various cuts. His life was in God's hands as he knew it always was, and he drifted off to sleep.

+

"I am Captain Tanner with the FBI and these are two of my detectives, Lieutenant Adams and Sergeant Ansel. We are here to track down a couple of felons that entered your country eight days ago. They are headed into the interior," Captain Tanner said with authority.

"May I see your passports?" the immigration agent said.

Tanner, Adams, and Ansel handed over their passports to the agent's outstretched hand.

"We're here with clearance from your Chief of Police, Jose Pena. He and Governor Branson from Texas worked out an agreement for us to enter and bring the fugitives back to the States," Captain Tanner explained.

The agent did not look up and appeared to be studying a notebook of some kind, flipping pages to look sincere.

"I know of no such clearance. There is no record of this in the files. Do you have some other documentation?"

"Listen, we need to go after these criminals," Captain Tanner reiterated.

"I cannot clear you through without the proper authorization, sir." The agent stood firm.

"Just call Pena. He'll know what to do, *comprendo hombre*?" Captain Tanner said sarcastically.

"Please come to the office, detectives. Follow me," the agent said while pointing his finger down a long, narrow hallway. "Follow me. This way, please."

Tanner and his two detectives followed the immigration agent down the florescent-lit hallway.

"This feels like a detention area, Captain," Sergeant Ansel said.

"More like interrogation," Lieutenant Adams insisted.

The immigration agent opened the door to the office and motioned for them to enter.

"Come in, detectives. Have a seat," a deep accented voice said in broken English.

The three Texas officers walked into the room. They looked around to see where the voice was coming from. On one side of the room, there was a crisp, dark brown leather couch, two cloth side chairs patterned in a fern fauna print, and two finely crafted teak end tables that each supported a designer crystal lamp. On the back wall hung a framed photograph of two men shaking hands and a Costa Rican flag in the west corner. Sitting on the corner of a table, on the other side of the room, dangling one of his legs over the side, was a man smoking a Cuban cigar.

The agent quickly closed the door behind them.

"May I get you boys something to drink?" the man asked.

"No thanks. What the hell is going on here? We need to see Chief Pena right away," Captain Tanner said.

"I am Chief Pena. How may I help you?"

"We need your authorization to go after some fugitives that entered your country last week. This was all cleared between you and Governor Branson. What's the holdup, anyway?" Captain Tanner asked.

"Oh, but you are mistaken my friend. I cannot let you chase after these people through my country like Texas cowboys with guns blazing. This is not allowed. We will escort you but only if and when we receive the trade agreement documentation from Governor Branson," the chief insisted.

"That could take days. They'll be long gone by then. You should take Governor Branson at his word and let us go in and do our job," Captain Tanner said.

"You and I both know Branson is not true to his word. He is a politician. I am sorry but you will have to wait until everything is signed off. I can have a driver take you to the San Clemente Hotel in Escazu, get you some girls. That is the best I can do for now." Chief Pena smiled.

Captain Tanner clenched his teeth. He knew they would lose their tails if they didn't get a move on it. "Is there a telephone I can use to call Governor Branson?" Captain Tanner asked.

"Be my guest. You can use the one down the hall in the holding area. I'll call my driver."

CHAPTER TWENTY-THREE

ANCESTUALLY

"We have to keep moving, Suneda. Negos will be waiting for us at Big Fork, then we can go home," Billie said.

"Our home, Billie, it will be our home."

"Yes, my love, our home. It will be a special resting place for Uncle Andy, too."

They both smiled at each other as they reached down to pick up their packs.

"Tell me more about your village, again? Billie asked. He wanted to forget about the broken body of his friend and focus on his life with Suneda. It was so close now, he could almost taste it.

"Oh Billie, it's one of the most beautiful places on

earth. The village sits at the bottom of a valley that is surrounded by the mountains. You can see many waterfalls cascading down hundreds of feet to the rivers and creeks that pass by the village. Sometimes after it rains, there are a multitude of rainbows dotting across the valley. In the morning mist you can smell the gardenias and the lavender," Suneda said with a smile.

"It sounds beautiful. What is it like at night?" Billie asked.

"At night, when the skies are clear, you can see a million stars. I've seen shooting stars too! You'll see fireflies and hear the croaking of the dart frogs."

"I can't wait to spend my life there with you, Suneda. I love you so much," Billie said.

Suneda smiled and gave Billie a sparkling wink.

They reached a small clearing on a riverbank about two miles downstream of where Andy had fallen. They unloaded and inflated the remaining raft. Soon after they cast off, the rapids started getting stronger, the speed of the river picking up. The sound of water slapping, swelling, and frothing against the rock walls was becoming thunderous.

"We are getting close, Billie. The fork is just a few miles now. We have to be careful. The rapids could tip us over at any time."

Both Billie and Suneda were fighting the rapids to stay upright, paddling in unison. The up and down, over and around motion made Suneda sick to her stomach again. She fought to keep her nausea down. Billie decided it was time to dock the raft and continue on foot. It was too late. The raft heaved hard left and straight up, tossing them both into the raging river. The contents of the raft, including all of their gear, was dispersed right along with them.

Billie grabbed a low hanging branch to hold onto. He saw Suneda's head bobbing up and down as she headed down the rapids a few meters down river from him.

"Get to the side! Get to the right side! There is a turn coming. You can get to the side," Billie pointed to the right as he shouted out to Suneda.

The water splashed over her head as she bobbed up and down. She grabbed some air when she could. Suneda heard Billie's directions and gave him a thumbs-up. She paddled hard with her arms but kept her legs up in a squatting position to stay upright and to keep her legs from banging or getting stuck on the rocks below the surface. She followed the natural current to a shallow swirling pool next to the river bank. She rolled over unto the embankment. Some of the contents from the raft were hung up in the cove, lapping around in circles.

Billie saw her land safely. He also saw the raft plunge over a gigantic waterfall just a few hundred meters from where they capsized. After a preview of what just happened, he let go of the limb he was holding onto and followed the same path that brought Suneda to safety.

"That was close, Billie. Thank you, Sibo. Could you see that waterfall through the trees winding back north of us? We would have plunged over to our death. We were lucky we fell in."

"I didn't think we could go much farther, anyway. The rapids are too intense for novice rafters, like us. I would much rather hike it on solid ground from here."

Suneda could not hold her upset down any longer. Billie rushed over to be by her side. He rubbed her shoulder and back.

"Let's rest here awhile. We will make it," Billie said.

✦

After a couple of hours, Jackie's ankle started feeling better. The salve Negos applied was working deep into the tissue and ligaments. It felt like her ankle was in a numbed freeze.

"What's in the salve, Negos?" Jackie asked.

"It is a local remedy made of forest herbs, used for generations by our shamans. It takes down the swelling and starts to heal the damaged tissue."

Negos also made a bamboo brace and walking stick that allowed Jackie to get up on her feet and continue their journey.

They arrived at the rendezvous point just before high noon. They were at the bottom shelf at Big Fork. Above them they could see the wood-slated bridge crossing to the other side of the gigantic ravine. Three rivers merged at this intersection: the Rio Saverage, the Rio Coco, and the Rio Baru, each one a little higher than the other, creating tumultuous waterfalls that crashed down around them. After the water from the rivers hit the shelf, it would pool before moving downstream. Crocodiles gathered at the pool, waiting for an easy meal to come their way. The food waste that littered the Rio Saverage from the village of Alta Vista above provided the crocs with a smorgasbord of chicken, tapir, and monkey bones.

"Thank goodness those things are twenty-five meters below us," Jackie said.

"Be glad they can't climb up slippery rocks," Negos joked.

"Not funny, Negos. Not funny. Those suckers are big," Jackie said, looking at the six- and ten-foot animals floating in the pool or sunning themselves in the sand.

Jorge looked down at the beasts and smiled. He was going to wait until the rest of them arrived before starting the "party."

✦

"What do you mean you're hung up in customs? Governor Branson said, obvious irritation in his voice.

"They are holding us up until the trade documents are signed off," Captain Tanner replied.

"I had a deal with Pena. Let me talk to that cheatin' weasel this instant."

Tanner handed the phone to Pena. Tanner cupped his palm over the speaker end so Pena couldn't hear the governor ranting and raving.

"Chief Pena here."

"Chief Pena, we had a deal," the governor blasted out.

"There is no deal until you sign the documents, Governor. I thought we were clear on that."

"You are holding up the pursuit of a dangerous felon that has entered your country illegally. Your president will hear about this," the Governor said in a huff.

"Governor, do not patronize me. You're pushing this for purely political reasons. My President knows you all too well. I take my orders from him," Pena shot back.

"Very well, I will get you the agreements this afternoon, and then I expect my detectives will be able to pursue this criminal without restraint."

Governor Branson slammed the phone down. He opened his desk drawer and retrieved the trade documents.

That bastard is not getting these now, he thought to himself. Then he pushed the button on the inner office intercom.

"Wanda, do you have my haircut appointment set up yet?" Governor Branson shouted.

⁂

Danny woke to the sound of howler monkeys foraging for food in the trees above him. It startled him at first, but then he relaxed as he watched a mother howler haul a baby along under her belly. His breathing was stronger and less painful. For the most part, his wounds had stopped bleeding. Thirst was driving his ambition to get his butt moving again. Having his wits about him now, he crawled over to a breadfruit tree and hiked himself up against it. *How many days have I been here*, he thought. And where is Jackie?

Is she looking for me or did she leave me for dead. "She must be looking for me," Danny prayed "She'll be here soon. She's my partner."

He pushed his back up against the tree and got up on his knees. With one arm still dangling, he squealed out in pain. Without hesitation he positioned his right shoulder so he could pop it back in place, then yelling out loud, he slammed himself into the ground.

Danny rolled on his back and tried to breath. When the initial pain subsided enough, he attempted to move his arm. It still hurt but he could tell it was now where it was supposed to be. He crawled gingerly, keeping the pressure off his left knee, to the river's edge where he gulped down water to quench his thirst. A ruffling noise above caused him to stop drinking. He looked at his reflection in the water. There, next to his own face was the image of a dark-skinned fat woman with long black hair. She was not the dreamy angel he envisioned coming to his rescue.

He rose to his knees and turned to face her. "Who the heck are you?"

She said nothing. She didn't seem to understand a word he said. She offered her hand to help him up.

"I guess you'll do."

She leaned back and jerked him to his feet.

"Ouch, that hurt like hell, lady," Danny said, wincing

as he hopped on one foot to stand up next to her. She stood in silence but allowed him to put his left arm around her shoulder and she began walking with him down an overgrown path heading away from the river.

"You're a little fat but as strong as an ox," he said with a smile. "I kinda like my women dark, short, and chubby."

She continued walking without saying a word.

Thinking the woman couldn't understand him, Danny thought he might as well have some fun.

"Maybe when I get better, we can have sex, rumba, rumba," Danny said raising his eyebrows at her.

She didn't even look up, she just kept on walking. A couple minutes later, she spoke.

"I guess you'll do. Better than nothing. You're kind of an ass but you're kinda cute," she said in perfect English.

Danny stopped walking. "I'm…I'm sorry. What's your name?" Danny asked.

"My name is Jemma."

"Nice to meet you, Jemma. My name is Danny."

They hobbled along in complete silence.

CHAPTER TWENTY-FOUR

EL COCODRILO

The Bridge at Alta Visa

Billie woke Suneda with a gentle kiss on the cheek. She rolled over and opened her dark brown eyes.

"It's time to go home, my love," Billie whispered in her ear.

Billie extended both his arms and pulled Suneda up to standing. He gave her a long, firm hug. They kissed. They held hands briefly, then started picking up their things.

"Soon we'll be home," Suneda said.

"It's a great day, Suneda. We'll leave the past behind."

Billie grabbed what was left from the raft and stuffed the items in his back pack. He noticed a strange object floating in the pool a couple of meters away. He waded into the water to retrieve it.

"I wonder where this came from," Billie asked.

"What is it?"

"It's a US passport. Name on it says Danny Logan. He's from Texas."

"That's strange. What are the odds of someone else from Texas being out here? I bet there are a lot of secrets in this pool. Do you think he went over the falls?" Suneda asked.

The thought of their near miss over the falls sent goose bumps up and down their spines.

They put their packs on and started their two-kilometer final descent to the shelf where they hoped Negos was waiting for them.

Only twenty minutes went by when Billie saw Negos waving to him from the shelf below, about twenty-five meters away. He got Suneda's attention and they both enthusiastically waved back. They slowly traversed the rocky slope to reach Negos and Jackie near the foot of the bridge.

"*Buenos dias*, Suneda and Billie," Negos said, pulling them both in for a hug.

"Who is this woman?" Billie asked, breaking the embrace.

"This is Detective Morris. She's a Texas Ranger. She has been ordered to take you back," Negos explained.

"We are not going back to Texas," Suneda said defiantly, her arms crossed.

"It's true, I came here to take you back. That's my job," Jackie explained.

"Do you know what we've been through in our lives, Detective?" Billie asked.

"I know both of your stories. We'll talk about this later. Right now we all need to get to safety," Jackie calmly explained.

"What are you talking about?" Suneda asked, quite confused.

"Someone's following us. We think he might have killed Detective Logan, my partner, two days back when we reached the Coco River fork. There looked like a scuffle and drag marks down to the water. There were no signs of Logan, not a trace," Jackie explained.

Suneda's skin became white as a ghost as she began to wonder if Jorge survived the plunge off Windy Bridge.

"What's wrong, Suneda?" Jackie asked.

"No way can it be Jorge, he fell from Windy Bridge. Our poor friend Andy tripped him off the bridge and Jorge fell into the Coco Rio," Suneda said holding back tears. "Andy saved us but later he died falling from the rocks above the river." Suneda started to sob.

"Calm down, Suneda. We saw Jorge fall to his death. I heard him hit. If that didn't kill him, surely he would have drowned. The rapids were relentless. Something else must have happened to this Detective Logan," Billie said.

"You did not find Jorge's body?" Jackie asked.

"No," Billie said.

"I don't know, Billie. I am scared to death Jorge

is still out there. And what about Andy? We're not one hundred percent sure what happened to him either. He fell from the summit. Did he trip and fall or did Jorge push him?" Suneda said almost in hysterics now.

"Calm down, Suneda, please. There is no way he could be in two places at the same time," Billie answered.

"El Sanguinio is invincible just like he said!" Suneda said sobbing.

"We're not sure what happened to Detective Logan, Billie. We thought it might have been Jorge, but we could be wrong," Jackie said before Negos could speak.

"What are we going to do?" Suneda asked, trying to calm herself.

"At this point we don't know if Jorge is alive or dead. We wanted to meet up with the four of you first and then figure out how to deal with this maniac. We should assume Jorge is alive and still wants his vengeance," Negos said. Then Negos realized Horace wasn't with them. "Where is Horace? Is he behind you? Did he turn back when you got close?"

"Uncle Negos, I hate to have to tell you but Horace was savagely beaten to death. This we know for certain. We found his body." Suneda began to cry again. Billie held her close.

"We killed him once, and if we have too, we'll kill him again. He won't be so invincible the next time I get my hands on the fucker," Billie said.

"We lost our guide to a puma and my partner, most likely, to this sick piece of shit," Jackie added. She checked her pistol to make certain the safety was off and it was still loaded. "I will kill him for you, Billie. He's mine. I owe that much to Danny," Jackie said with confidence.

"We found Mr. Logan's passport in the river. You might as well take it, Detective." Suneda handed Jackie the passport.

"Let's get out of here. We'll go into Alta Vista and get some help from the locals," Billie said as they all stood up to move on.

"This is the way" Suneda pointed to the north.

"We're only a few kilometers from my village. Leave the packs here." Negos said. "We'll come back and get them later. We only have a couple of hours of daylight left. I don't want us to be out here at night with a sociopath."

Having heard enough, Jorge lunged out at Detective Morris from behind a bolder. He dislodged the gun from her holster and pulled it out of the sleeve, pointing it directly at Jackie. Then he swung the gun around to Billie, stopping his advance, then over to Suneda and back again to Jackie. They were all afraid to move, unsure of where Jorge would strike first.

"Don't worry about going back to Texas. You're all going to die here, except you, my sweet Sunny girl; you're going back to Mexico to spend time with my friendly associates. You'll wish you were dead when they are finished with you," Jorge said with a seething glance at Suneda.

Suneda kneeled down and cupped her hands over her face.

"I am going to kill you, you son of a bitch," Billie shouted.

"Sure you will, tough guy. Will that be after I pull out your fingernails and rip your teensy weensy balls off or after I cut your throat and drink your gringo blood? I am El Sanguinio the invincible. Surely you know that by now. You stole my woman and now you must pay with your life, it's that simple," Jorge said, his eyes bulging out from their sockets.

He threw Negos some rope and instructed him to tie up the others. One by one Negos tied them up as told. Jorge kept the gun cocked and pointed directly at the back of Negos' head in case someone tried doing something stupid.

When Negos finished tying them all up, Jorge ordered him to walk over to the ledge above the crocodile pit. He knew what Jorge had in mind, so he stumbled to the ground, coughing and wheezing.

"Get up, you good for nothing Boruca trash."

Jorge grabbed the back of Negos' shirt and kicked him closer to the edge. Negos grabbed a handful of dirt and gravel and rose up halfway and threw it into Jorge's face. As Jorge wiped at his face, Negos reached for the gun. It went off as it hit the ground and flew over the ledge. The crocodiles were stirring now.

Agonizing pain shot through Negos' leg and he screamed out in pain. He grabbed his thigh where the bullet had entered just above his kneecap. He was bleeding rapidly.

Jorge saw his chance and pushed Negos off the ledge too. Negos screamed as he tumbled down to the crocodile den below. The dinner bell had rung.

Jorge turned back towards his three captives and was startled to see they had almost escaped. Billie had already untied Suneda. Jorge ran up to him as he was attempting to untie Detective Morris and cold cocked him in the side of the head. It knocked him off balance and Billie fell over and hit his head on the rocky ground, losing consciousness. Suneda rushed over to Billie's side and tried to wake him.

"Billie, wake up! Billie!" Suneda shouted.

Jorge grabbed Suneda by the hair and dragged her away, screaming and kicking.

When Jorge looked up, he was surrounded by ten or more men. "What the fuck…Who the fuck are you people?" Jorge asked, dumbfounded. He released his grasp enough on Suneda that she was able to break away.

Twelve more villagers stepped out of the brush and circled around him as though he was a tapir in the middle of a hunt. Wielding his machete, Jorge lunged back and forth at them, assessing the villagers' resolve. He shouted profanities at his attackers while poking his machete at them. The circle of villagers tightened around him.

"Back off or I'll kill all of you," Jorge screamed as he looked for an escape route. He was surrounded. The crocodile pit was to his left. A steep cliff was to his right. Detective Morris was still tied to the tree, and Suneda was kneeling over an unconscious Billie.

The villagers moved in closer. They began banging the sticks in their hands.

"I will not be taken alive. I am El Sanguinio. I am invincible. Do you hear me? I am invincible!" Jorge shouted.

Chief Yanto came to the forefront. He held a two-foot machete above his head.

"I am Caciqua Yanto, leader in my village. Who are you that you come to hurt my people?"

Jorge did not speak. He was still looking for a way out. He began sweating profusely. Suneda left Billie and ran up to the chief.

"Father, Father, my dear Father!"

Chief Yanto looked at Suneda in bewilderment; he thought he was seeing a ghost.

"You are alive…My little princess, you have come home to me. We thought you were dead. We thought you fell to your death crossing Big Fork," he said, wrapping his arms around Suneda.

"Yes, Father, I'm alive. I know what I did was wrong but I am here to stay now. This is where I belong. This is where I need to be. My path took me home."

"Who is this wild and crazy man before me?" Chief Yanto asked her.

"This is the man who has stolen my dream to become a doctor in America. He has violated me. He almost destroyed my life. He is pure evil," Suneda said, pointing a shaky finger at Jorge.

"I have heard of this El Sanguinio animal. He has brought his evil drugs to many of our countrymen. He has caused much heartache and destroyed the lives of so many of our people," the chief said.

"So you admit you are El Sanguinio? You did these things to my princess?" Chief Yanto asked Jorge, looking at him with pointed anger.

"Yes, little monkey-man. I am the great El Sanguinio. What are you and your little Indians going to do about it? Have you not figured out that your blood is mine. All of you are mine."

Then without warning, Jorge charged at Chief Yanto swinging his machete wildly. The chief sidestepped, letting Jorge pass him by.

Nimbly, Jorge got hold of Suneda again, grabbing her by the hair and dragging her toward the rain forest with his machete firmly pressed against her neckline.

"Billie, Billie! I need you, Billie!" Suneda cried out in desperation.

"Shut the fuck up, bitch. There is no one who can help you now. I'm going to slit your throat and drink your blood in a toast to your memory," Jorge yelled out. He pressed the blade against her skin, drawing blood.

Hearing Suneda's scream, Billie woke. He saw the horror show unfolding twenty feet away. Ignoring the pounding in his head, Billie rose to his feet. Everything was spinning, but he stumbled toward Suneda, landing squarely at the feet of El Sanguinio.

"How may I help you?" Jorge chuckled.

Billie stood again, eyes squinting to focus.

"This fight is between you and me. Let Suneda go," Billie demanded, his hands in tight fists.

Jorge just laughed.

The villagers moved toward them, but Chief Yanto raised his machete.

"Back off or I kill her right here, right now!" Jorge yelled.

The villagers backed off. An odd expression played across Jorge's face. "I did tell Sunny I would kill you right before her eyes. Let her watch you die, slowly. I must keep my word or what good is my word?" Jorge said, his features oddly relaxed. He hurled Suneda violently to the ground and stepped up to Billie.

Chief Yanto tossed Billie his machete. The circle enlarged as the villagers enclosed the two men.

Billie lifted the machete in a defensive move as Jorge took a full swing with his. The metal of the two machetes clashed behind the weight of the two fighters causing them to both lose balance and fall to the ground. Jorge was the first one up. He charged at Billie as he tried to rise. He knew he was no match for Jorge in his present condition, his strength was useless now. He had to think of another way to defeat this madman. Then Billie saw it, his way out. He dropped his machete and put up his hands in defeat.

Jorge stopped and stared at the big man at his feet. "You finally realize my power," Jorge said, then laughed.

Billie stood and teetered, moving backward as if he was going to fall. Jorge followed him, his arm out ready to push Billie over. Billie grabbed Jorge's arm and dropped on his back. He planted his foot in Jorge's stomach and pulled him over his head. Jorge landed on the ground above Billie's head and at the base of a tree.

Jorge screamed as if he were being stabbed. He scurried to his feet and began swatting at his legs. Hundreds of small reddish-black ants were crawling all over Jorge's legs.

"*Hormiga Vienticuatro*," Suneda whispered in horror.

On their trip through the jungle, Billie had put his pack in a nest of these ants when he set it up against a tree. They were called bullet ants or twenty-four ants by the locals because if you were bitten, it took twenty-four hours of horrible pain to get over their bite. He was about to brush them off when Suneda rushed over to stop him. She had explained to him that this small creature had the most painful bite known to man and if you were allergic to its venom, it could kill you.

Billie rolled a few times to get out of Jorge's way and away from the ants. Everyone stood back as Jorge continued to scream in agony and slap at the small creatures, not paying attention to his surroundings. It was too late when he discovered he was too close to the ledge. He fell over, into the crocodile pool just as other villagers were pulling Negos out. The crocodiles had lost one meal but gained another.

At the moment Negos hit the water, a large, gray crocodile charged at him, its mouth wide open. Negos was able to hold its jaw open just a few seconds, before it clamped down on Negos' hand. The crocodile pulled him under the water, trying to drown him. They resurfaced and went back under half a dozen times. A couple of other crocodiles were circling around them, waiting to get a piece of the action.

Negos began to lose consciousness when four villagers jumped into the pool with spears and knifes. They stabbed at the crocodile repeatedly, but its hide was as coarse and tough as boot leather. Plus they didn't want to hit Negos. Finally, a spear penetrated the beast's soft belly, and the crocodile instantly let go of Negos and swam away. The villagers let the crocodile go and dragged Negos up onto the bank. He wasn't breathing, and he was missing his left hand.

Another man fell into the pool as they left the water with Negos. This man was farther out and they had a harder time getting at him. He was dead and missing a leg by the time they got him away from the large reptiles.

CHAPTER
TWENTY-FIVE

INCESTRY

"Wake up, Negos. Do not leave us!" Anale yelled, then started mouth-to-mouth resuscitation. "Wake up," she repeated. Negos' heartbeat was slow. His body was cold.

"Hold on, Negos. Hold on. Do not leave me, my love." Tears streamed down Anale's face as she continued to blow into his mouth.

Negos coughed up water and opened his eyes wide. Anale turned him on his side as he continued to cough water out of his lungs.

When he finally caught his breath, he couldn't believe who was at his side: his beloved Doctor Oliver. He thought he had died and gone to heaven. Negos smiled and grabbed hold of her, wanting her to be real.

"Anale, you are here," Negos said, his eyes filling with tears.

"Negos, my love," she said and kissed him on his forehead, then held him tight. "I am here and so are you."

Negos soon drifted into unconsciousness in Anale's arms. She helped some of the villagers hoist him onto a palm-frond gurney to take him back to Alta Vista.

After Doctor Anale Oliver made sure she could not help the other man in the crocodile pool, she headed for the bridge. Anale had someone else she had to see.

⤙

Suneda ran over to Billie's side. "Jorge is dead. My monster is gone. You killed him, Billie," Suneda said joyfully. She wrapped her arms around Billie and kissed him.

When Suneda eventually let go of him, Billie touched the knot that was protruding from his forehead He stood up, but his world was still spinning. He tried to keep his balance.

"Billie, Billie, my sweet little Billie. It's me, your mother." Anale came running up to him and jumped on him almost tackling him back to the ground.

"What are you talking about?" Billie snapped back.

"I am your mother. I've been looking for you since you were a baby. My God, I can't believe I found you. You are right here in front of me," Anale said as she touched his face, his hair….

Billie could see the resemblance in her facial features. The light blue eyes, contrasting with the dark brown, wavy hair left no doubt they were related.

Billie stepped back. He had dreamed of this moment for a very long time and yet he couldn't believe she was here and outside of Alta Vista. "What the hell? Is it really you? I thought you left me. I thought you gave up on me. What are you doing here?"

"Yes, it's me, Billie. I never stopped searching for you. I could never do that." Anale's eyes began to tear up.

Suneda started crying. Billie started crying. The three of them embraced each other, seeming to never want to let go.

Chief Yanto and Detective Morris stood close by.

It took a while but they finally let go of each other.

Suneda turned to Chief Yanto. "Father, this is my Billie, and this is his mother, Elana. She was lost and now she is found," Suneda said, soaking up her tears with the sleeve of her shirt.

"Just like you, Suneda. You were lost and now you have come home," he said, and he kissed Suneda on the forehead.

He turned to Anale. "Welcome back to you as well Doctor Oliver...I mean, my dear Sister-In-Law." The chief hesitated before he went on. "Do I know Billie's father?" Chief Yanto asked.

"Yes, Chief. Negos is Billie's father."

Billie closed his eyes and held his head. This was all too much. He leaned over, then fell, unconscious.

"We need to get him to the village and tend to his injuries," Chief Yanto said as he motioned over to a few villagers. Four men picked up Billie and took him into Alta Vista.

Jackie looked over the edge to see what had happened to Jorge. Suneda stepped up next to her. The villagers stood around his lifeless body and looked up at them, unsure what to do. "I suppose we will have to come back later to bury his sorry ass," Jackie said to Suneda.

"No, we will not. We will let the chicken hawks, beetles, and worms eat his evil soul, what's ever left of it," Suneda said as she walked next to Billie.

CHAPTER
TWENTY-SIX

MR. JACAB

Governor's Mansion
Houston, Texas

"Wanda, book me a flight to San Jose, right now. I have a meeting with President Ortega tomorrow afternoon," Governor Branson shouted from his office.

Wanda rolled her eyes, then stepped into his doorway. "Would you like to stay at the Intercontinental Casino Hotel in Escazu that you like?"

"Of course. You know the drill. Put the Holiday Inn on my itinerary but book the Intercontinental."

"Yes Governor," Wanda said softly. Governor Branson was such a hypocrite. He had voted against a bill to allow gambling in the state, but he never lost an opportunity to play cards when he could.

You are such an ass, she thought and turned to leave.

‑✧‑

Sierra came running up to the procession as they entered the village. They started chanting a tribal rhythm once they reached the edge of the village.

"Suneda, Suneda, my baby!" Sierra yelled, tears streaming down her cheeks.

Suneda ran up to her mother and gave her a big hug. They embraced for several seconds, rocking back and forth.

"Mother, I have missed you so much. I have been through so much. I was wrong to leave. Please forgive me," she said with tears in her eyes.

"You are home now. You are safe. That's all that matters now," Sierra told her daughter, still holding her hand.

Suneda pulled Sierra towards Billie. Someone had run ahead and brought back a gurney for him to lie on. They were taking him to the medical clinic.

"This is my Billie. And this is Billie's mother, Elana Jensen," Suneda told Sierra.

"Elana? You mean Anale, Doctor Oliver?" Sierra said with a confused look on her face.

"Hello Anale. I see you are back," Sierra said a bit disgruntled.

"He still has a slight fever. His pulse is strong though," Doctor Oliver said while smiling back up at Suneda and Sierra.

"Doctor Oliver, thank you for your help. We must all put the past behind. You will always be welcome here," Sierra told her.

Chief Yanto walked up to them as his wife was talking.

"Yes. This is your home too, if that's what you choose. Negos is my brother. You are now a sister. You have a son so Billie is my nephew. We are happy he is home as well. We are family. All is forgiven," Chief Yanto told her.

"Thank you, Chief, but my first priority is to get Billie and Negos to the clinic where I can tend to their injuries. Negos has lost a lot of blood and needs many stitches for his wounds. He is in stable condition. I gave him a sedative and a pain killer back at the river. He will rest now. He is a strong man and a fighter. Billie is in a coma. I suspect he has some swelling in his brain. I need to set up an IV drip and monitor his vital signs every four to six hours."

"How long will he be in a coma?" Sierra asked.

"It could be a couple of hours, a few days, or maybe months. We need to keep him as comfortable as possible. As long as Billie's vital signs are strong, we don't need to worry, we just need to be patient," Anale explained.

"I need to check you over too, Suneda. You have been through a lot," Anale said.

"*Si*." Suneda couldn't argue.

✦

"Tanner, what the hell is going on down there? Have you heard from Detective Morris or Logan? I got media all over my ass up here," Warden Stackhouse yelled over the phone.

"Not a peep from either. I am stuck down here in San Jose with two of my deputies. We are being watched as though we are two-bit criminals. They have a detail on us, for Christ's sake," Captain Tanner replied.

"Don't they know who the hell you are?" Stackhouse questioned.

"It doesn't matter. They don't give a damn. They won't release us because they are waiting for Governor Branson to keep his word on some kind of trade deal, but I can't help but feel like that's not all of it."

"We might be screwed. Branson has never kept his word on anything unless it benefits him politically."

"They told us Branson is coming down tomorrow for a meeting with President Ortega to work it all out. In the meantime, my boys and I are going to drink heavily, roll some dice, and play some blackjack."

"Lucky you. In the meantime, I get to tell the news people and all the other sick fucks around here, I don't know shit."

"Better you than me, Stacky. Better you than me," Captain Tanner said while chewing ice and gurgling down his scotch with a pretty girl sitting on his knee.

"Just keep me in the loop. You got it, Tanner?" Warden Stackhouse said, then he slammed the phone down.

"I am so fucked."

✦

"Suneda, I need to speak with you," Detective Morris said as they were leaving the village clinic where Billie and Negos were recovering.

"We are not going back to Texas, if that is what this is about," Suneda told her.

"No, I don't expect you or Billie ever will, Suneda, but I need to close this investigation and I need your help to do it. Anale is going to San Jose for more medical equipment and supplies later today when the air transport gets here. You'll come with us. We need to talk to your grandfather. We have a plan."

✦

The trio arrived in San Jose before Governor Branson and his security team. The governor's entourage would plug up the airport for hours, buying them some time to plead their case. They hurriedly hailed a taxi and headed to the presidential palace. The last time Suneda was in San Jose, she was ten years old, six years before she ran off to the United States for a "better" life. Her grandfather had been newly elected the Mayor of San Jose and she and her parents had gone to help him celebrate his victory. The outlying villages had a voice in the government for the first time ever.

The entrance to the government house was spectacular. Bougainvillea, mandevillea, hibiscus, gardenias, and coconut palms lined the driveway all the way up to the steps of the big white house. Her grandfather was now the president of Costa Rica. Suneda was so very proud of him, but she was just as ashamed for what she had done to herself and her family name.

Jackie broke the silence as they were driving through traffic. "I've heard he is a fair man, Suneda."

"He is a fair man. He is also a wise man," Suneda said.

"He will understand then?" Anale questioned.

"He will protect his family and his country," Suneda said.

As they approached the security gate, a large man with a cane came out to greet them.

"How may I help you?" he asked.

"We are here to see President Ortega. He is my grandfather. I am Suneda Ortega."

"Little Princess Suneda. Is that you? I haven't seen you since you were about ten years old. Everyone thought you had fallen off the bridge at Big Fork and died in the rapids. Your grandfather grieved for days."

When the man smiled, she instantly remembered his big gold tooth. It sparkled back at her just like it did when she was a little girl. He was always by her grandfather's side.

"I am sorry for running away, Mr. Jacab," Suneda said solemnly.

"Does your family know you are here and that you are alive?" he asked.

"Yes, everyone except my grandfather."

"He will be happy to see you and know that you are alive. Come this way." He waved the three of them along with his cane down a narrow winding path. They arrived at a large bronze double door that Mr. Jacab opened with a key. It opened to a flower-print-walled foyer with high ceilings and a crystal chandelier. To the right was a social seating room. The room was adorned with paintings of all sizes and shapes. Portraits of important people hung above four fireplaces. There were couches, cocktail tables, and settee' groups arranged throughout the room. Each cocktail table had a vase full of Bird of Paradise. Wall-to-wall windows faced out to the west garden that had almost every plant native to Costa Rica in the landscape accented by a series of small, rock waterfalls and ponds.

"Come right this way, ladies. Have a seat anywhere you like. Make yourself comfortable. I will get the president," Mr. Jacab said.

They looked around the room in amazement. The artwork and local artifacts all around the room were outstanding pieces of culture and history.

A few minutes later, President Ortega entered from a side door.

"Suneda, my dearest granddaughter, Suneda!" he

said, his arms flung wide. "You are among the living! Come give me a hug," President Ortega said with his eyes fixed on Suneda.

"I know, Grandpapa. I am so sorry I did this to you and my beautiful family."

"We have much to catch up on. You will stay with me for a few days before heading back to the village. I insist."

The president turned to the other women. "Which of you is Detective Morris?"

Jackie nodded her head. "That's me, sir. Pleased to meet you," she said and held out her hand.

He shook it politely. "Now Detective, what is this urgent matter you need to discuss?"

✦

Governor Branson's plane was delayed three hours because of his large security entourage, taxpayer funded, of course. He always felt the bigger his security team, the more important he was.

When his team landed, Chief Pena was there to escort the governor to the presidential palace. His security detail flanked him on both sides as they headed off the tarmac.

"So you're the fella holding up my boys from doing their job down here, hey Chief," the Governor said as they shook hands.

"A deal's not a deal until the paperwork is done, Governor. You and I both know that," Chief Pena told him in a businesslike tone.

"I know son. Don't get your pants all wadded up. It's just business. It's just politics, my boy," Branson joked.

Chief Pena now knew why he didn't like Governor Branson.

"Follow me this way to my car, Governor." the chief escorted him to his Mercedes Benz stretch limousine.

"Not doing too damn bad for yourself, young man. Business must be good here, goddamn it. I should think about moving down here," the governor said laughing out loud as he slapped Pena on his back and tipped his Stetson hat in approval.

CHAPTER TWENTY-SEVEN

THREE FINGERS PROOF

Alta Vista

Negos was starting to feel better. His wounds were recovering nicely from the crocodile bites and he felt lucky to have lost just a hand.

Negos was concerned about Billie as were the rest of the villagers. It had been months since he fell into a coma. All of his vital signs were strong; he just wasn't ready to wake up.

Doctor Oliver told them he would be fine. He just needed more time. His body and mind were healing. Occasionally, Billie would toss and turn and shake around violently, his nightmare surfacing. He had to be subdued with arm and leg restraints so that he would not hurt himself. Suneda knew he was reliving his nightmare. There was nothing she could do but be there for him and feel his pain. She could still visualize Jake Jensen molesting Billie. It made her sick. She was proud that Billie took charge of his life before Jake would have killed him. She was glad he was with her in Alta Vista. She prayed each day he would wake up to his new family.

"Thank you for meeting with us, President Ortega," Jackie said.

"It's my pleasure, Detective Morris. It is you who must be thanked."

Detective Morris had made the decision not to bring Billie back to the US authorities. She had a plan to save face for everyone. She just had to sell it to the president. Suneda and Anale were there to back her up as needed. They explained everything that happened to Suneda from the day she left. Suneda detailed her encounter with Jorge and how he kept her captive. They talked about Jake and Billie. Anale explained her relationship with Negos and that Billie was their son. They spoke about the journey to Alta Vista and how El Sanguinio stalked them and was killed by Billie. They told him about Billie being in a coma.

"I see. All of you have been through a lot. We have quite a mess to sort out. Governor Branson from Texas will be here shortly demanding we allow his team to pursue his escaped convict, our Billie, or extradite him back to Texas if he is in our custody. We have a trade deal tied to this matter. This is most important to our countrymen," President Ortega said.

"You have a much bigger bargaining chip in your hands than you may think, President Ortega. I know how Governor Branson thinks and works. It's all about politics to him. Let me explain my plan," Detective Morris said.

✦

The limo pulled up onto the circle driveway in front of the presidential palace. The two security-detail SUVs pulled in right behind it. One of the secret service men raced over to open the passenger door to let the governor out. Chief Pena got out on the other side as the driver opened his door.

"Well, ain't this the place. Maybe Texas should annex it," Governor Branson said as he surveyed the grounds surrounding President Ortega's home.

The door to the palace opened and Mr. Jacab came out to greet the governor.

"You must be Governor Branson," Mr. Jacab said with his arm extended to accept a handshake.

"I am Mr. Jacab, President Ortega's chief of staff."

"It's nice to meet you, Mr. Jacab. I am looking forward to getting my prisoner back," Governor Branson said as he shook his hand.

"Right this way, Governor." Mr. Jacab led him up the steps to the front door.

They walked down a long carpeted hallway and entered a large office. In the center of the room was an oval conference table.

"Governor Branson, please have a seat and make yourself comfortable. I will summon the president. He will meet with you here. Would you like something to drink?" Mr. Jacab asked.

"I'll have a Johnny Walker on the rocks with a splash of water if you don't mind; it was a long flight," Governor Branson said with a slight grin.

"As you wish, Governor. Chief Pena, will it be the same for you?"

"Make it straight up for me. It's been a very long day," Chief Pena said with one eye closed.

Chief Pena took a seat on the opposite end of the table from of the governor. Pena wanted to be as far away from this Texas asshole as possible. The governor gave it no notice.

When President Ortega entered the room, there was an awe of silence. Even Branson took notice of the commanding presence of the president as he walked toward him and Chief Pena.

"Governor Branson, welcome to my home and my country. *Siéntase como en su casa*," President Ortega told him as he reached out his hand.

"Please sit, Governor. We have much to discuss. I see Mr. Jacab has already tapped into the thirty-year-old scotch. Did he tell you we reserve it for only our finest dignitaries?" President Ortega said.

"Thank ya'all, Mr. President. It is as smooth as the silk on the underside of a sow's belly." The governor chuckled, sipping the whiskey. He wasn't sure what the president had said in Spanish, so he just nodded his acceptance, figuring he meant no harm.

"Well, I am glad you approve, Governor. Now sir, what brings you here to meet with me this fine day?"

Chief Pena and the president were looking at each other, wondering how the hell it was that this idiot got elected.

"We've got a bit of a problem, Mr. President. You've got one of my convicts on the run here in Costa Rica. Out there in that damn jungle of yours. I need your permission to pursue him and bring him back to Texas to face justice, Texas justice," the governor said boldly as he looked directly into President Ortega's eyes.

"I know of this convict, Governor. Chief Pena here and one of your detectives have already filled me in. His name is Billie Jensen. Is that correct?" President Ortega asked.

"Yes, that's him. So you know where he is? Give him to my Texas Rangers and I'll be on my way. The tables are waiting for some blackjack to be played." The governor was surprised they already knew something about Billie Jensen. *This is going to be this easy*, he thought.

"Do you know of his story?" the president asked him.

"I don't give a shit about his story. I have my political

ass on the line here. You know how this goes," Governor Branson stated outright.

"Easy does it, Governor Branson. Billie Jensen is in our custody and since we do not have a formal extradition treaty, I am afraid you can't have him. At least not until we do a thorough review of his case," President Ortega said.

The governor's face turned red. He was clearly getting upset. "Review his case? What the hell. How the damn long is that gonna take? Sounds like a fishing trip to me," the Governor blurted out in a slightly slurred Texas drawl.

"As long as I say it takes," the president said.

"Well, that sleeping dog don't hunt by me, Mr. President," Governor Branson said, clearly irritated.

President Ortega and Chief Pena looked at each other simultaneously with puzzled looks on their faces.

The governor regained his composure when he realized he wasn't making sense.

"I guess the trade deal I had with Pena is off, Mr. President," the Governor said confidently as he slammed his glass on the table in an attempt to get their attention.

"You have to deal with me Governor, not Chief Pena. He answers to me. Chief Pena, please excuse us while the governor and I speak privately."

"Yes, Mr. President, as you wish," Chief Pena said. He stood and walked to the door.

"Please sit down, Governor. I think we have a solution that will be politically beneficial to both of us," the president said as he shut the office door behind Chief Pena.

"Let's have a seat over here on the sofa. Would you like another drink?" the president asked as the governor meandered over to the sitting area.

"You are talkin' Texas talk now, and as ya'all put it that a way, of course, another Johnny W is just what the presidente ordered. A double, please, no cubes," the governor said as boldly as ever. He knew something was in his favor when the president sent Pena packing.

Suneda, Anale, and Detective Morris were patiently waiting in the foyer for the outcome of the president's meeting with Governor Branson.

"Are you going to tell the president he is going to be a great-grandfather?" Anale asked.

Suneda looked up at Anale surprised. She was only in her first trimester and she wasn't even showing. *How did she know?*

"Of course I will, in due time. He will be so happy. This will be his first great-grandchild," Suneda said solemnly as she touched her belly.

"It's even more important now than ever that we protect Billie from being sent back to the United States," Jackie said. She was now one hundred percent behind Billie and Suneda's new life.

"*Si*," Suneda said.

"Yes, we must do whatever it takes for Billie to be finally free to live his life. I lost him once and I will never let that happen again," Anale said.

"I need my Billie back. I need him to wake up." Suneda cupped her hands to her face to muffle her cries.

Anale touched her hand. "He will be fine, Suneda. Maybe he will be awake when we return to Alta Vista. We must keep the faith. Let's pray," Anale suggested.

With that said, the three of them joined hands and bowed their heads in silent prayer. When they finished, the door to the executive office opened.

The president and the governor were laughing and joking with each other as they exited the room. The president had his hand on the governor's shoulder. They acted as if they were the best of pals.

The three ladies stood at attention to greet Governor Branson. Chief Pena was off to the side observing.

"Governor, this is my granddaughter, Suneda Ortega," the president said as he walked the governor over to her. He shook her hand with authority.

"And this lady next to her is Doctor Anale Oliver. She is Billie Jensen's mother," the president said, continuing his introductions.

"It is very nice to meet you, ladies," the governor said with a smile.

"And you must be Detective Texas Ranger Morris," Governor Branson said.

"Yes. I am Detective Morris, Governor. It is nice to meet you, sir."

"The president told me you have a gift for me, is that correct? May I see the picture?" the governor asked.

Jackie reached into her backpack and pulled out a crumbled yellow manila envelope and handed it over to the governor. The governor reached inside and pulled out a Polaroid picture of El Sanguinio, the most wanted man in America, dead as dead can be. The envelope also contained a flock of hair and three of Jorge's fingers wrapped tightly in a plastic bag for final identification purposes.

"I'll be damned, Ranger Morris. You've got us three real prizewinners here. Good work, Detective," the governor told her as he dangled the bag of digits in her face.

"The governor and I have come to an agreement. The State of Texas and the Costa Rican government, with the support of Governor Branson and his Texas Rangers, in coordination with our police force, apprehended and then in a bloody escape attempt, killed the most vilified and feared outlaw of our time. They will bring part of this monster's body back to Texas and take credit publically for his demise. In exchange, Billie Jensen will not be extradited to the United States. It has been determined that Ms. Anale Oliver, aka Elana Jensen, gave birth to Billie before she returned to the United States, making Billie a natural born citizen of Costa Rica and, therefore, not extraditable. He is Billie Ortega now. His fate will be determined by my executive order. Did I miss anything,

Governor Branson?" the president said to his captive audience.

"No sir, Mr. President. Ya damn well covered it nicely. I could not have said it any better myself."

"In addition, we have a new trade agreement in place, lifting the tariffs off our produce and coffee and chocolate exports to the State of Texas in exchange for an exclusive oil purchase contract from Texas. Is that correct, Governor Branson?" President Ortega confirmed.

"Yes sir, Mr. President. You got it right. We are Texas proud to partner with the people of Costa Rica to make our economies stronger," the governor said as he hand rimmed his cowboy hat.

CHAPTER TWENTY-EIGHT

WHO'S BARU?

Billie was tossing and turning in deep sleep. The nightmare of his stepfather's abuse was recycling over and over in his head.

Yeah.. yeah…the monster's dead…yeah, yeah… Bang, bang.

He was trapped in his dream and could not wake up to free himself. He was breathing heavy. The sweat was dripping off his entire body. Negos was wiping him down with a cool towel to comfort him. He was not going to lose another son. He prayed Billie would awaken, for five months had gone by and he begged his savior daily.

"Please, Father in heaven, help my Billie. Bring him home to us safely. I know I have done terrible things in my life, but I have changed. He is my son. I need him here with me," Negos pleaded to Sibo.

Then finally as if to answer his pray, Billie woke up briefly then went unconscious again. Sibo was listening. The others in the room were silent. Anale always said it was critical for Billie to wake up slowly until he gathered all of his senses. Negos whispered for someone in the room to go get Suneda and the others.

He turned back to his son. "Billie, please wake up my son. I am your father, Negos. No one here will ever hurt you again. Come back to us," Negos said quietly as he rubbed Billie's arm.

Billie moaned as he tried to lift his arm. He squinted, trying to open his eyes. He blinked several times as if he was trying to focus. Billie's nose picked up an intense smell of gardenia in the air as the breeze picked up and wafted through the room. This time he could see a fuzzy figure hanging over him. He knew it was Negos from his deep raspy voice. Billie opened his mouth and moved his lips as if to speak. Nothing came out, only a few grumbles of noise. Negos hunched down over Billie's face and moved his ear up close to Billie's lips.

"It's all right, Billie, take your time. You have been in a coma for many months. We've been waiting for you," Negos said with excitement. He was now rubbing Billie's arm faster.

"Negos, is that you?" Billie said in a whisper; talking seemed awkward to him. He also felt the presence of others surrounding him. He could hear them breathing. All of his senses were coming into focus at the same time.

"Yes, it's your father, Negos," Negos said gleefully. The others gathered around to catch a look at Billie waking up. They poked their heads in, biting their lips to not make a sound.

"What? What do you mean? What are you saying?" Billie said. His skull still throbbed and even hearing his own voice hurt his head.

"Billie, it's me, Suneda. I am here with your mother, Elana. Detective Morris is here with Mary Smithers and Doctor Scott. And...I have a very special young man for you to meet," Suneda whispered in his ear as she leaned over and gave Billie a kiss on his cheek.

Billie was still disoriented and somewhat confused. He had no idea he had been out for so long. As soon as he recognized it was his beloved Suneda, he smiled at her. His heart filled with joy.

Suneda proudly laid a newborn baby in the crook of Billie's arm. "This is your son, Billie. His name is Baru."

Billie eyes opened wide. He was fully awake now. Suneda and Anale helped sit Billie upright. Billie gazed down at his son in amazement and held him on his chest, close to his heart. He could feel the baby breathing and hear his heart beating. Billie was overwhelmed with joy and a happy peacefulness set in.

"My son, my father, my mother...my God I am confused. Sibo where are you?"

Everyone laughed.

"What are you telling me? My mother is here with me and my father is Negos?" Billie said, looking at all the smiling faces around him.

"Yes, it's me, Billie. We still have a lot to talk about. We all do. Get your rest now," Anale insisted as she took her grandchild from him and squeezed him tightly.

"Wait a second, Mother, before Billie takes a rest. I have one more person for Billie to meet and for Jackie to see," Suneda exclaimed.

"What? Who for me?" Jackie asked puzzled.

"Who is it now?" Billie asked.

"Wait one second. I'll be right back." Suneda quickly left the room and exited the clinic.

After a few minutes, Jemma, a woman in the village, came into the room with a long-haired, bearded man. The man was leaning on a boa-head capped bamboo cane. Silence engulfed the room as everyone focused on the door.

"Holy shit, you son-o-bitch Danny, is that you?" Jackie blurted out. "I am going to kick your sweet butt," she said, stepping up to him. "Give me a big hug you perverted meathead of a partner you."

"Good luck with that, my dear. My ass is already taken!" Danny said with a snake-eating grin on his face as Jemma looked on.

THE END

Acknowledgments

To Theresa my partner in our journey through this life together. I could not have done it with out your full support.

To Christine Keleny for her patient counsel, professionalism, editing and publishing expertise.

To Jack Ewing for sharing his vast knowledge of Costa Rica, it's people and the indigenous Indian tribes.

To the Boruca people, who shared their village with me during their festival – The Dance of the Diablos.

To Skip Nall for the perfect Brige to Alta Vista photograph.

To Rosemary Stark for putting her attention to detail on proofing the manuscript.

To my friends Melissa Jackson and Nikhil Melnechuk for their encouragement and support.

To my friend John Buffalo Mailer for his coaching, idea sharing and editing assistance.

To the many blessings that have been bestowed upon me and the opportunity to live and play in the beautiful idyllic lands and waters of Costa Rica.

About the Author

Born and raised in Michigan, Gerald attended Western Michigan University where he received his Bachelor of Business Administration Degree in Marketing and Business Communications. He moved his family to Houston, Texas in the 1990s where he built a successful business. An entrepreneur turned novelist at 58 years old, Gerald has traveled extensively throughout Mexico, the Caribbean and Central America. In 2008 he bought a villa in the rain forest area of Dominical, Costa Rica where he traveled throughout the country for many years, getting to know and understand the beauty, culture and the Tico people of Costa Rica. The inspiration for the purely fictional work *Bridge to Alta Vista* came to light one day on a flight back to Houston over the expansive Talamanca mountain range where way way down below sat a remote village of the Boruca Indian people. These people live a life of self-subsistence, completely off the grid with a tribal-like reliance on one another for basic needs and survival. This village still exists today. How could that be? Who are these people? Why do they live this way today? Why do they stay, or do they choose to leave?

Bridge to Alta Vista is Gerald Thompson's first novel

and has been adapted and optioned to Winding Roads, LLC to be considered for a feature film. Look for its release in 2019-2020.

Book reviews for *Bridge to Alta Vista* are always welcome. Please submit online or visit:

www.geraldthompsonauthor.com

Other books in the works by Gerald Thompson include:

The Silent Stalker and The Three Mushrooms, a psychological mystery thriller

Sea Grass, a suspense thriller

www.ingramcontent.com/pod-product-compliance
Lightning Source LLC
Chambersburg PA
CBHW021419110726
47901CB00008B/2217